ronald rabbit is a dirty old man

D1225425

ronald rabbit is a dirty old man

lawrence block

subterranean press * 2000

First Subterranean Press Edition
January 2000

ISBN
1-892284-56-1

Subterranean Press
P.O. Box 190106
Burton, MI 48519

Website:
www.subterraneanpress.com

Email:
publisher@subterraneanpress.com

The earth is flat.

Mrs. Lisa Clarke
219 Maple Rd.
Richmond, VA.

Dear Lisa:

I trust you've already established that there's no check in this envelope. No matter how long this letter turns out to be, no matter how many sheets of paper wind up folded together and stuffed into this envelope, the first thing you'll do is shake everything out looking for a check, and there won't be one. So you've done that by now, and you said, "The dirty rat bastard said he'd send a check and there's no check here and this better be good."

I'll make it as good as I can, Lisa.

But where to start? Why, at the beginning of this beautiful day, dear Lisa, when Laurence Clarke sprang out of bed with a smile on his lips and a glint in his eye and—

Oh, hell.

Rome must have fallen on just this sort of day. A bright sun shining, a ghost of a breeze toying with the garbage in the gutters and plucking the hems of the mini-skirts, even the air pollution in the acceptable range. I actually hummed on the way to the office. Hummed! And some of the people I passed in the streets were smiling. Genuine New Yorkers with discernible smiles on their faces. I know it sounds impossible, but they couldn't all have been tourists. Some of them must have been natives, and here they were smiling at one another.

Extraordinary.

I picked up a *Times* in the lobby, let the elevator levitate me to the twelfth floor, helloed and nodded and—yes—*smiled* my way through the outer office, and was at my own desk with my own door snugly closed by five after nine. I spent half an hour reading the paper. There was nothing particularly ominous in it,

7

for a change. I finished it and chucked it into the wastebasket, opened a desk drawer and got out my current book, a first novel by a young person who had distinguished himself in several student riots before entering the world of letters. The publisher and a variety of critics were spread all over the dust jacket, applauding the author for telling it like it is.

Yecchhh. The book was a 300-page refutation of the Winston commercial—it proved you could sacrifice good grammar without even approaching good taste. The person (the author's name was sexless, and the dust-jacket photograph sexually ambivalent) threw words about like paving stones, and all he told me was that verbal communication may well be obsolete after all.

(But not for us, Lisa the formerly-mine. By God, woman, I'm enjoying this! Do you know I haven't written this much in a couple of years? All these words winding up on all these pages, and all with no discernible effort on my part. I just sit here at this typewriter and let it all hang out, as the children say. Are you my Muse, Lisa? And are you amused, Lisa? I *know* you'd rather have the check—)

Ah, well. I went on slogging my way through muddy prose until ten-thirty, slipped downstairs for coffee and prune Danish, came upstairs again and read some more until lunchtime.

I lunched with a friend who has an expense account. Do you remember Bill Adams? He's over at Ogilvy now, doing something that sounds boring enough. Got married about two years ago, I think it was, and just last month bought a home on the Island. We went to an Italian place on Second Avenue and ate cannelloni and killed a liter of red while I listened to him talk about how great it was to be out of the city and how his job seemed secure although half the advertising business was on the beach and how much he loved his wife and what a good marriage they had going. He talked and I listened and he paid and I burped and we left, and it was still the same beautiful day outside.

Then he said, "Listen, you don't have to go back to that office, do you? I mean, not right now. Because there are these two chicks with an apartment just around the corner, and it's a shame to be in the neighborhood without dropping in on them. What do you say?"

"Hookers?"

"Well, they get twenty, so you couldn't call them virgins. But nice girls. One of them used to be a stewardess."

"What did the other one used to be?"

"A virgin, I guess. I used to be a virgin, come to think of it. You game, Larry?"

I said I couldn't afford it.

"Oh, shit," he said. "You're making good dough."

"I have two wives to support," I said. "One current and one former."

"I have one wife and one house. Believe me, a house is worse than a wife in that respect, past or present. I have crab grass to kill. Come on, I hate to sin alone."

"You're happily married," I said.

"What the hell does that have to do with it?"

"I don't know."

"Don't tell me you don't fuck around."

"So?"

"Christ, I'll *loan* you the twenty."

I thought about it. "I just don't really feel like it," I said. "Look, it's not as though you can't go alone. What's the problem?"

"I'll tell you, I get very awkward going there alone. Because there's the two of them."

"So?"

"So I hate to choose between them. It's like rejecting one of them. It's like picking one and telling the other 'You're a nice kid but I'd rather fuck your roommate.' So she's rejected, and she sits in the other room watching the fucking television set, and the whole thing puts me off stride."

"You're putting me on."

"I just don't like to reject people."

He was serious. I looked at him thoughtfully. "Go to bed with both of them," I said.

"Huh?"

"No rejection. Take them both to bed, lie there in the middle and ball them both. So it costs you forty instead of twenty and you kill a little less crab grass next week."

"Jesus," he said. "You ever do that?"

"Kill crab grass?"

"Two girls at once."

"Yeah," I said. "Not hookers, and not recently, but yeah."

"Is it great?"

"The only problem is that it can sometimes get hard to keep your mind on both of them at the same time. For me, anyway. I'm generally better on one-to-one relationships. But with paid talent I don't think it would matter that much."

His jaw set and he gripped my arm. "You're a brother," he said. "I'm gonna do it."

"Hang loose."

"I will. You're a prince, Larry, I mean it. We'll have lunch again soon. Call me."

"I will."

"My love to Fran."

"And my love to Paula."

He looked at me. "Their names are Bunny and Aileen," he said. "Aileen was the stewardess."

"And Bunny was the virgin, I know. Paula's your wife, schmuck."

"She's a wonderful girl," he said automatically. "She really is, Larry. She's good for me."

I went back to the office and tried reading some more, but I kept imagining myself lying between a former stewardess and a former virgin, one of them asking me to be gentle and the other offering me coffee, tea or milk. As I pictured them, the stew looked a lot like Fran and the virgin looked a lot like Jennifer. (I never told you about Jennifer, did I?) I'm sorry to say that neither of them looked like you, Lisa. You do worm your way into my fantasies from time to time, but you weren't in this one. Sorry about that.

Then my phone rang.

This wasn't alarming. I have this phone on my desk, and now and then it rings. Sometimes it's Fran asking me to pick up something on my way home. Sometimes it's Jennie wondering if I can duck out on Fran for a couple of hours that evening. Sometimes, God help us, it's you, wanting to know why the alimony check hasn't turned up yet.

So it was a beautiful day, and my phone was ringing, and I picked up the phone, and in my little world the sun hid behind panther-colored clouds, the carbon-monoxide and sulfur-dioxide levels soared, the stock market sank without a trace, and the sword of Damocles began its swift descent.

"Laurence Clarke? This is Mr. Finch's secretary. Mr. Finch would like to see you in his office."

"In his office," I said. I have a tendency in moments of stress to repeat the last three words of other people's sentences. When Fran and I were married, I said "Help you God" instead of "I do." Which gave a few people a few bad moments until I corrected myself.

"Yes," said Mr. Finch's secretary.

"Now?"

"Now, Mr. Clarke."

Yecchhh.

Mr. Clayton Finch's office is on the fourteenth floor, which is one floor above the twelfth. Clay Finch is not, as one might understandably guess, a target for particularly adept skeet shooters. He is in fact the president of Whitestone Publications, the fount from whence flows a torrent of paperback books and magazines of no particular distinction. In this capacity he has been, for just less than ten months, the employer of yours truly, Laurence Clarke.

He looked more like a cast-iron owl than a clay finch, anyway. He gazed at me over his desk, all eyes and a couple of yards wide. His was a much larger desk than mine, and his office, unlike mine, had windows. Several of them. Let it be known, though, that I in no way begrudged him these trappings of status. I was perfectly content with my little desk and my airless cubbyhole and my subsistence-level salary.

"Laurence Clarke," he said.

"Mr. Finch," I said.

"Laurence with a U," he said. "Clarke with an E."

"With an E," I echoed.

He closed his eyes. He opened them, and he shook his head sorrowfully from side to side, and then he closed his eyes again. "I suppose you ought to sit down," he said.

I sat down.

"You've been with us since September," he said. "You were hired as the editor-in-chief of *Ronald Rabbit's Magazine for Boys and Girls*. We pay you"—he consulted a scrap of paper— "a salary of $16,350 annually."

I nodded.

He picked up a pipe, turned it around and around in his manicured hands. He said, "*Ronald Rabbit's Magazine for Boys and Girls* suspended publication with its January issue. I suspect the publicity had something to do with it. Your predecessor Haskell; even though we fired him, the story couldn't be hushed up. An eleven-year-old boy, for heaven's sake. And then offering the defense that the boy told him he was fourteen. A bad hat, Haskell. And the scandal inevitably rubbed off on *Ronald Rabbit*."

"It hardly seemed fair," I put in.

He sighed. "You prepared the December and January issues," he said. "After which time the magazine ceased publication. Since then you seem to have continued to come to your office every day, Monday through Friday, except for a week's vacation in April and four days in February when you were ill."

"Asian flu."

"You've continued to draw your full salary. You're listed in the books as the editor of this *Ronald Rabbit* thing." His eye focused thoughtfully upon me. "Mr. Clarke," he said, "just what on earth do you do?"

I swallowed, but that didn't seem to answer his question. I said, "Uh, I get a lot of reading done."

"I imagine you do."

"And I, uh, keep myself available."

"Whatever for?"

"For anything that might come up."

"No doubt." He closed his eyes for a longer period of time. He opened them and sighed, perhaps because I was still there. "It must be very boring for you," he said. "Doing absolutely nothing, day after day, week after week, month after month."

"Month after month," I said.

"Eh?"

"I haven't minded it, Mr. Finch."

"Is that so?"

"Yes. Of course at first I hoped someone would find something for me to do, but after a while I began to get used to it. To having nothing to do, that is."

"You never went looking for another job."

"No, I've been happy here."

"And you never tried to find anything else you could do here?"

"I didn't want to call attention to myself."

He winced. "Eight months of well-paid inactivity," he said. "Two months of work and eight months of total sloth. I've never heard of anything like it. Do you realize what you've done, Clarke? You've stowed away on a corporation."

"I never thought of it that way."

"It's quite incredible. When this came to my attention I was fully prepared to be furious with you. For some curious reason I find myself unable to work up any genuine rage. Astonishment, yes. Even a sort of grudging admiration. I have to admit that I found myself looking around for something else you could do for us. But of course there's nothing open. Everybody in the industry is busy reducing staff these days; combining jobs, eliminating deadwood. You're the deadest possible sort of wood, Clarke. No offense intended, but you're the rottenest limb on the Whitestone tree."

I didn't say anything. Neither did he, so I finally broke the silence. "Then I'm fired," I said.

"Fired? Of course you're fired."

I nodded. "I knew it would have to happen sooner or later. It was too good to last."

"Fired? What else could you *be* but fired? Promoted, perhaps? Rewarded with a raise?"

"I'll miss working here," I said. To myself more than to Finch.

He stood up. "Oh, we'll miss having you, Clarke. I don't know how we'll get on without you." He started to chuckle, then broke it off sharply and resumed the head-shaking routine. "Well," he said, "I've had a check drawn. Your salary through today plus two weeks' severance pay and six days' sick leave." He picked up a check and frowned at it. "Of course you weren't here five years or you would have been participating in the profit-sharing plan. Suppose you'd stowed away for five years? Or forever? The mind boggles. Well, I don't suppose it will take you long to find something suitable. We'll give you a good reference, needless to say. We've had no complaints about your performance of assigned tasks, have we?"

I laughed politely.

"And in the meantime you can begin collecting unemployment benefits. A comedown from your present salary, but your duties will be essentially the same."

"Essentially the same." I took a breath. "Could you tell me how you happened to, uh, find out about me?"

"Your expense account," he said.

"My expense account?"

"Part of the current austerity program. I had someone going over expense-account records for the past half year to see who might have been taking a bit of advantage. And your records immediately attracted attention."

"I never used my expense account, Mr. Finch."

"Precisely. An editor who doesn't charge a minimum of three lunches a week to the company stands out like a sore thumb. Surprising you weren't detected earlier. Why, you should have been gouging us for an extra twenty-five or thirty dollars a week at the least."

"It didn't seem honest," I said, thoughtfully.

"Honest," he said. "Well," he said. "I won't keep you, Clarke. You'll want to clean out your desk. If there's anything in it. And you'll want to say good-bye to some of your co-workers, if you've happened to meet any of them in the course of your stay here. It's been a pleasure, Clarke. An educational experience."

We shook hands. I said, "If you should ever decide to reactivate *Ronald Rabbit*—"

"Oh, we'll keep you in mind, Clarke. We'll certainly keep you in mind. Count on it."

I got back to my own desk and sat at it and thought how I was going to miss it. I had a check in my pocket for almost a thousand dollars. There was another hundred in my wallet and something like fifteen hundred in our joint checking account. In a drawer at the apartment, there were bills running to perhaps a thousand dollars. Fran earned $130 a week before deductions, considerably less after them. Presumably we wouldn't starve, with her salary added to my unemployment. Not right away, at least.

But what was I going to do?

It was a very weird moment or three, Lisa love. A very weird couple of moments indeed. Larry Clarke, Laurence with a U and Clarke with an E—and wouldn't it be nice, by the by, to have a name one didn't have to spell for people. Laurence Clarke himself, a poet whose Muse went into retirement a year and a half ago. Born thirty-two years and ten days ago, a Gemini with Scorpio rising and Moon in Leo. Unemployed, and presumably unemployable. A lad with talents unexciting enough in a booming labor market, and here we were in a labor market that could hardly have been less booming. If the economy got a little worse I could respectably sell apples on street corners, but what would I do in the interim?

Consider this: In all my life I had only found one job that I truly and unequivocally enjoyed, and now I was fired from it.

I picked up the phone and called Fran's office. She had not come in to work, someone told me, nor had she called in. I tried her at home and the phone rang for a while before I gave up on it.

I decided it was just as well. Conversations with Fran had been difficult enough lately, even when I had good news. But I had to talk to someone, so I called Steve Adel. Of course you remember Steve, old college buddy and best friend in all the world. Best man at our wedding, you recall. Best man again, when I married Fran. He's still in photography, has a loft of his own on

Centre Street. He wasn't around, though, and I sat there trying to think of someone else to call, and the phone rang, and although you might think I'd have know better, I answered it.

A collect call from Richmond, Virginia. There is only one person who calls me collect, and only one person I know in Richmond. Both of those people are you, Lisa. I accepted the call on behalf of Whitestone Publications—it was all I could do to compensate them for not having made use of my expense account. And there you were, as you perhaps remember.

You may remember the conversation as well, but I'm going to reproduce it here just for the sake of continuity.

> LISA: Sweetie, it's good to talk to you.
> LARRY: You've eloped.
> LISA: No, honey —
> LARRY: You've moved up the wedding, though.
> LISA: (*Giggles deep in her throat. There was a time, you know, when I loved the sound of that giggle. There was also a time when I wanted to be a fireman when I grew up.*) No, just the opposite, lover. Last night Wally and I called the whole thing off. No wedding bells for Lisa.
> LARRY: No wedding bells.
> LISA: 'Fraid not. Oh, it just wouldn't have worked out, honey. Just no way. He's a sweet guy and I do love him some, but as far as marriage goes, no, it just couldn't have worked out for us.
> LARRY: You don't want to jump to such an important decision, Lisa.
> LISA: Oh, be sure I gave it mucho thought, honey.
> LARRY: I see.
> LISA: But there is no way to make it work. Oh, we're fine in bed, lover, but that's just not enough to build a marriage around. As far as that goes, you and I were good in bed, Larry. I can still say that you were one of the best lovers I've ever had.
> LARRY: I don't know how to thank you.

LISA: Of course we were both a good deal younger then. You've probably learned a lot more since those days. God knows I have.

LARRY: I can imagine.

LISA: Can you? But as far as marriage goes, I think it can go without me. Honestly, darling, there are times when I think I'll stay single for the rest of my life. So I'm afraid those alimony checks won't stop next month after all, sugar. As a matter of fact —

LARRY: I was fired today.

LISA: Fired?

LARRY: Today. The magazine ceased publication, so they let me go. So as far as the checks are concerned —

LISA: Oh, I'm sure you'll be able to keep them coming.

LARRY: You are, eh?

LISA: I have confidence in you. But this does change things, doesn't it? You see, Daddy has been after me to increase the checks. He says with the way inflation is going, and the increase in the cost of living...

(I missed a lot of what followed there, Lisa. When you quote your father you talk the same legal bullshit he talks. But the gist of it seemed to be that the old bastard wanted you to petition the court for an increase of a third in your alimony payments.)

LISA: (*Cont'd.*) But of course this changes things. I still consider myself your friend, lovie, and what are friends for if not to be understanding in times of stress?

LARRY: Times of stress.

LISA: So we'll just let it stand at $850 a month until you get things straightened out. I just hope you won't be unemployed for too very long.

LARRY: So do I, actually.

LISA: Oh, just incidentally, I didn't get this month's check yet. I suppose it's in the mail?

LARRY: You know how the mails are.

LISA: But I suppose it'll get here within a day or two, don't you think?

LARRY: You'll get your money.

LISA: I'm sure I will, doll.

LARRY: But I wish to hell you would marry the son of a bitch.

LISA: Men are supposed to be upset when their ex-wives remarry. A virility-anxiety thing, I think it is. They don't like to be replaced. I read that many of them even enjoy paying alimony, that they get their kicks out of the measure of control it lets them keep over their ex's life.

LARRY: You read that, huh?

LISA: It makes sense, don't you think? Except for those men who don't have much virility to be anxious about.

LARRY: I've got to go now. My other phone is ringing.

LISA: Fun-nee.

LARRY: It was good talking to you, Lisa. It always is.

LISA: Sometimes I think it's a shame we didn't work out, Larry. But we had some good times, didn't we?

LARRY: Some good times. No argument there.

LISA: How's Fran?

LARRY: Fine.

LISA: Give her my love.

LARRY: Will do.

LISA: Bye, hon. And don't forget the check, huh? I'm kind of broke.

LARRY: I won't forget.

Outside, away from the air conditioning, the weather had gone to hell along with the rest of my life. It had turned hot and damp, and the air was foul. I took a taxi. Pecuniary emulation, your father would call it. Spending money unnecessarily because one lacks it. Ego food. Whatever the reason, I couldn't hack the subway.

Bleecker Street had never looked bleaker. I dogged it up the stairs through the cooking smells and let myself in.

Nobody home. I had a drink and was building another when I found the note. It was on the kitchen table, and I suppose I must have looked at it several times without seeing it. The work of a benign Providence. Obviously God knew I ought to have a drink inside me and another close at hand before I read that fucking note.

I reproduce it for you, Lisa:

Larry:

I can't go on living a lie. Steve and I have been lovers since March, and everything has grown ever more intense. No doubt you've noticed I've been acting strangely lately and I guess that explains why.

By the time you read this we will be on our way to Mexico. We will stay with friends of his in Monterrey for a few weeks and will probably wind up in Cuernavaca. Steve has been wanting to photograph the ruins.

Cowardly of me, I know, but I couldn't face telling you all this. Nor could I help doing it. Thanks for some mostly good years.

With some (but not enough) love,

Fran

P.S.—I closed our checking account.

I went around the corner to the bank, and she was right. The checking account was gone. I sat down with a vice-president and we figured out how many checks were outstanding and cashed my final Whitestone check and put in enough money so none of the checks would bounce. I wound up with a couple of hundred dollars. There were still all those bills upstairs, and I still owed you $850, Lisa, the very $850 which I am not sending with this letter. The bank officer asked me if I wanted to open a new account; I decided to keep the money in cash. Not that I would be keeping it very long.

Then I came back here and finished the drink, and then I read Fran's letter a few more times.

Friday, June 12th. It should have been the thirteenth. I had just lost my job and my wife and most of my money. I had retained my ex-wife and the privilege of defusing my virility-anxiety by paying her four times as much each month as I would receive in unemployment compensation. The only person I really felt like talking to about all of this was on his way to Monterrey with Fran. (And why, I wonder, did the silly cunt insist on furnishing me with their itinerary? Could I look forward to a parade of postcards? *Having wonderful time. X marks our room. Wish you were here.*)

I called Jennifer, who lives on East Seventh Street and weaves rugs and tapestries. We have an undemanding sort of relationship, Jennie and I. I drop over there once or twice a week and we smoke a little grass and listen to a little music and fuck a little. I told her I was at loose ends, which was as true a statement as any I have ever uttered, and that I thought I might go over and see her.

"I don't know," she said. "I'm kind of uptight. I just got my period yesterday and I had this hassle with the super and I'm in a shitty mood. If you just wanted to talk a little and watch me weave—"

Jennifer is twenty-two, with a supple body and pale skin and long mahogany hair and trusting acidhead eyes. All of this makes her a yummy fuck but a verbal nothing. Going over to her place just for conversation is like going to a Chinese restaurant just for dessert. This is all right on grass—ten-minute silences aren't bothersome then—but I felt not at all like getting high. I wanted to close the doors of perception, not open them.

And what's deadlier than watching someone weave?

"Maybe some other time would be better," I said.

"Actually, we *could* ball. Not balling during your period is just a hangup, you know. You probably wouldn't want to go down on me, but—"

"It's not that," I said, truthlessly. "I'm uptight myself. I think the vibrations would be bad."

Jennie is one of those young female persons who will accept any explanation that has the word *vibrations* in it. She agreed that we would make it another time, and I picked up the phone again and tried to think of somebody to call. Or someplace to go. Or something to do. And managed to think of none of these things.

I came very close to calling you, Lisa, as a matter of fact. The only thing that stopped me was that I didn't want to hear your voice. I don't mean that quite the way it sounds. I had some things to tell you, but I didn't want you talking back to me while I tried to get it all out.

So I decided to write a poem, and set the typewriter upon the kitchen table, and rolled a sheet of paper into it, and spent a long time looking at it. Which made it as close as I had come to writing a poem in about a year and a half.

And then I thought, well, I can't send Lisa a check, and I'd better tell her as much before her father sends his bloodhounds after me. Does the old bastard still raise bloodhounds? I'm sure he does.

So I started to write you a letter, and I seem to have gotten carried away. Ridiculous, isn't it? All of this just to tell you that there's no check in the envelope, when you found that out before you read a word.

Christ, Lisa, I've written twenty goddamn pages of this. I can't believe it. This stupid letter is the first thing I've written in a year and a half. It is already longer than either of the two attempts I made a writing novels, and probably more cogent than either in the bargain.

All those months at *Ronald Rabbit's*, with a desk and a chair and a typewriter and nothing but solitude, and I never wrote a fucking word. And here I am beating this typewriter to a pulp, the words just rolling straight from my brain through my fingers and onto the page. Pages. Page after page after page.

Lisa, Lisa, Lisa. We did have some good times, damnit. We truly did. And I think it's nice we haven't let the fact that we sort of hate each other keep us from loving each other a little.

Ah, Lisa. Here's your letter, and I'm sorry there's no check to go with it, but there isn't, and God knows when there will be. You don't have to answer this letter. You don't even have to keep it. I have a carbon. I just never did get out of the habit of keeping carbons of things, and when I first put the sheet of paper in the typewriter I hoped it would turn out to be a poem. But maybe this is better. The world has enough poems, and maybe it needs more prose.

Anyway, I've solved a problem. When I started this I didn't know what to do, and now I do. I'm going to tuck this into an envelope and go downstairs and mail it, and then I'm going over to the Kettle to get drunk.

You may be hearing more from me, Lisa.

With love (but without $850),

Larry

74 Bleecker St.
New York 10012
June 15

Mr. Stephen Joel Adel
c/o American Express
Monterrey, Mexico

Dear Steve:

Let me tell you in front, old pal, that I think you're a total rat bastard and an unprincipled son of a bitch who ought to be tied up and horsewhipped.

Now that we've got all that out of the way, I thought I'd write and tell you and Fran how I've spent the past couple of days. As she may have told you, Fran was considerate enough to leave a note, and it seems only civil of me to respond to it. I originally thought of writing to Fran instead of to you, since it was Fran and not you who left the note for me. But I rolled this sheet of paper into the typewriter and stared at it and, instead of typing "Dear Fran," I typed what you see above. This sort of thing has been happening lately. I started to write a poem Friday afternoon, and what came out was a letter to Lisa. You remember Lisa.

Why didn't you ever take *Lisa* to Mexico, you son of a bitch? Christ, I would have paid your plane fare.

Anyway, the point is that I've decided not to fight my typewriter. Whatever it wants to do is fine by me. I spent a year and a half deep in writer's block, and now that I think about it I can't avoid the suspicion that it happened because I would sit down at the typewriter with certain preconceptions that kept getting in the way. I would decide to write a certain poem, and that poem just wouldn't happen on the page, and as a result I didn't write anything for a long time, until I decided to short-cut the whole operation by not sitting down at the fucking typewriter in the first place.

You picked a good day to take yourself and Fran out of my life. I got home early that afternoon because they canned me at *Ronald Rabbit's.* They finally figured out that I was a captain without a ship, and instead of finding another ship for me they cut me adrift and let me swim. You'd love the story, but I've already written it all to Lisa and I don't want to go through it again. It wasn't that much fun to live through, let alone to write about. If you ever have an affair with Lisa (after all, there are only three hundred people in the world, and sooner or later they all sleep with each other), maybe you can get her to show you the letter. Or if you ever meet Clay Finch, he'll give you his side of it.

I got home from *Ronald Rabbit's* with my cottontail between my legs, and found that you had hied yourself south with my wife and my fifteen hundred dollars. I know it's ungallant as all hell for me to say this, and you may not want to show this part of the letter to Fran, assuming you want to show her any of it, but of the two, I rather miss the fifteen hundred more. I had a use for it, what with a drawer full of bills and alimony to pay and no money coming in. I had a use for Fran, but we must face facts. If one takes a walk down the street, one has a much better chance of picking up a woman than of picking up fifteen hundred dollars.

An even harder thing to pick up this late in life is a best friend. Much as my first impulse was to hate you, I've decided it would be silly to throw off a fifteen-year friendship over something like this. At the moment you're near the top of my shit list. There's no getting around that. But I know that you have a sense of honor, and sooner or later you'll send back the fifteen hundred and all will be forgiven. If, on the other hand, you keep the fifteen hundred and return Fran, I swear I'll hunt you down and cut your fucking throat for you.

Jesus, I hope this letter gets to you. I don't suppose you were expecting mail, but if I know you, you'll check with American Express in every town you hit, whether anyone knows you're going to be there or not. And Fran is just about as compulsive that way. I think I'll put something on the envelope about forwarding it to Cuernavaca if you don't call for it in two or three weeks. Fran said (well, *wrote*, actually) that you wanted to go to Cuernavaca to photograph the ruins.

I didn't know there were ruins in Cuernavaca. For that matter, I didn't know you had this big thing for photographing ruins. If you wanted ruins to photograph, old buddy, you didn't have to go all the way to Cuerna-fuckingvaca to take pictures of them. You could have come over to Bleecker Street and worked your shutter to the bone.

In fact, precisely that notion was going through my mind when I finished the letter to Lisa. I put a lot of stamps on it and mailed it, and then I went over to the Kettle of Fish and behaved as though they were going to reintroduce Prohibition on the morrow. I drank Irish whiskey for a while, and then I drank some India Pale Ale. Do you remember the time we got totally wiped out on India Pale Ale at the Riviera, and we wound up taking this cab full of conventioneers to Harlem and pimping for them? Of course you remember, how could you forget, how could anybody forget?

Ah, those were the days, Steverino. . . .

I didn't get totally wiped out this time, however. I kept on drinking, gradually slowing the pace and letting myself get wrapped up by first the jukebox and then some old thoughts. I'd planned on devoting the major portion of the evening to self-pity. In fact I was looking forward to it. But self-pity is like cops and cabs and women—it's never there when you want it. I would try to tell myself how classically desperate my situation was, how absolutely everything had gone wrong at once, even to Jennifer having her period.

I know that you know about Jennifer, but I don't know whether or not you told Fran. I was wondering about that as I sloshed down the India Pale Ale, as it happens, and I tried to put myself in your position. If I were fucking the wife of my best friend, I asked myself, and if I happened to know that said best friend had an occasional piece on the side, would I tell the best friend's wife about it? I could see one good reason to do so. It could lessen her guilt, after all. I mean, cheating on a cheater is just turnabout, which we all know is fair play.

But on second thought, I decided that if I were fucking my best friend's wife, the last thing I would want to do is cut down the guilt. I mean, man, without the guilt, what would be left of your relationship? You can both feel guilty about how you're giving the shaft to old Laurence with a U, Clarke with an E. Your mutual guilt holds you together, no? The day you begin to exorcise my ghost, the day there's just the two of you in that bed without my ectoplasmic presence to keep you company, that's the day you two will begin to fall apart.

I'm a sneaky son of a bitch, aren't I?

Ah, well. If you haven't told Fran about Jennifer, you might as well tell her now. I'm glad I told you, Steve, and I'm also glad I never introduced you to Jennifer or you might have taken them both along to old Me-hee-co. Who steals a man's wife steals trash, but he who steals a mistress—

Speaking of trash, I have a thing to tell you, Steve, and I don't know how to do it without violating the bounds of good taste. The thing is, even without self-pity, I did find myself thinking a lot about my relationship with Fran. Naturally I was seeing it in a new light now. For something like three months she had been having an affair with you, and I was just now learning about it.

(Incidentally, where did you screw? Our apartment or your loft? It's hard for me to believe that you spent all that much time together. Fran didn't have too many unexplained absences. Oh, well. If you ever reply to this letter, you might let me know how you worked out the mechanics of the affair. I find myself oddly, even dispassionately, interested in that sort of thing. God knows why.)

What I realized in the Kettle, though, was that although I never suspected anything at the time, anything at all, I could in retrospect almost put a date on the beginning of your affair with Fran.

It must have started just about the time she wouldn't swallow.

Oh, hell. There's no way to be tasteful about this. And I could not mention it at all, but the typewriter tells me it wants to discuss it, and I already explained about giving this typewriter its head.

And that's what this anecdote is about, anyway. The giving of head.

Well, I don't suppose I have to tell you that Fran gives sensational head, Steve. You probably think the girl is a born cocksucker. Actually, I can say with a certain amount of pride that I taught her virtually everything she knows in that department. When I first meet your mistress, Steveroo, she was a far cry from the Oral Vacuum Cleaner she is today. Oh, she was willing enough to play the flute, you understand, but she kept hitting the wrong notes. But a willing pupil, God knows, who ultimately earned the title Miss Million Dollar Mouth. As a matter of fact, it was her skill in this area which moved me to propose marriage, and at the actual moment when I popped the question (among other things) she was physically incapable of answering, her parents having schooled her not to talk with her mouth full.

Good taste does seem to have gone by the boards, doesn't it?

But one evening in March, probably a day or two after you two commenced your playlet of star-crossed lovers, Fran and I went to bed, and stroked and petted in the usual fashion, and then I crouched on hands and knees and paid oral homage to the little man in the boat. (We had gradually weeded *soixante-neuf* out of our repertoire, on the theory that it was better to concentrate on one thing at a time.)

Fran had herself a nice hearty orgasm. I'm sure she didn't try to tell you that she and I stopped balling in the course of her affair with you, but it's possible she fed you some shit about not having orgasms with me, or faking them. I wouldn't blame her for that lie, and neither should you, Steve. Just a white lie, after all. And I don't imagine you would have been stupid enough to believe it, anyway. You know what Fran's like when she comes. All those delicious contractions, and the subtle taste of egg white. She could no more fake that than Vesuvius could counterfeit an eruption.

When the lava stopped flowing, I flopped on my back like a beached whale and let her return the favor. No point in describing all that. No doubt you're as familiar as I am with the ministration of those lips and that tongue.

Ah, I shall not entirely cease to miss you, Fran—

But to the point. She did her work well, as always, and I got where I was going, and then she inexplicably began gagging and coughing and ran to the toilet, where she relayed my gift to her to the New York sewer system. The toilet flushed and she returned with a vaguely troubled look in her eyes, muttering something about something having gone down the wrong way.

I don't think we screwed any less frequently after that, Steve. She never pleaded a headache when I was in the mood, and as a matter of fact, she occasionally initiated things. But she stopped swallowing. I wish there were a couther way to say it, but there isn't. She stopped swallowing.

Funny how there are levels to intimacy, isn't it? An echo of adolescent dating behavior, when there were things one could do on a first date and other things one could do on a third date and still other things one could do only when one was truly in love. We all of us have different levels, different cutoff places. Some women with a far lower threshold than our Fran would find it impossible to sleep with two men at the same time. Others would find it possible to engage in the act, but could only achieve orgasm with one of the two partners. Others might manage intercourse with both lover and husband, while withholding fellatory delights from the latter. But this adorable girl has yet another set of standards. Her lips were never sealed, just her esophagus.

Why am I telling you all this? I'm sure you can guess my baser motives, but there is one altruistic impulse involved as well, old buddy. If you two are going to live together, you ought to know as much as possible about one another. And you also ought to be able to know when someone has begun to replace you in her affections.

The day she spits you out, old buddy, is the day you've been replaced.

This typewriter is really chock-full of surprises. I honestly never meant to write you any of this. I didn't mean to write you at all, as I said. I was going to write Fran and tell her how I spent the weekend. When one has been jilted, one wants to get a little of one's own back, ignoble as that may be, and this was a sensational weekend, and writing to Fran about it would constitute a symphonic chorus of "I can get along without you very well, believe me. . . ."

Believe me.

I left the Kettle when they closed it, since there didn't seem to be any alternative. By then I had drifted in and out of perhaps a half-dozen conversations and twice as many private reveries and was having a high old time, in all senses. And I had very nearly managed to drink myself sober all over again. To wit, my memory of some of those hours in the Kettle was sketchy, but when I walked out into the stale air of MacDougal Street I was in full possession of what faculties Providence gave me.

Not that I was sober. I could walk straight and talk straight and think straight—well, almost—but I was nevertheless looped.

If drinking always worked that way, I swear I'd do it every night. There'd be no earthly reason not to.

So I walked up MacDougal Street singing something. I think it was "Big Yellow Taxi," the Joni Mitchell thing. There are some difficult notes in the chorus and I was missing some of them, and aware of it, but I still sounded pretty good to me. I crossed MacDougal at Third Street. I don't recall having any special destination in mind. There was a station wagon waiting for the light to change. I crossed behind it (which I suppose constitutes jay-walking, which you can add to the list of my sins) and I paused at the end of a line of the song, suddenly unable to remember what came next, and through the open rear window of the station wagon two voices supplied the next line in unison. Two clear, fresh, youthful, soprano voices, and they got all the notes right.

I leaned an elbow on the back of the wagon and peered owlishly in at them. The car was full of girls. There was one in front driving and one sitting next to her, and there were two more in the back seat, and there were another two—the songbirds—sitting cross-legged in the luggage compartment. The ones that I could see were all very pretty. So, I learned later, were the others. A total of six pretty girls sitting two and two and two in a station wagon at the corner of MacDougal and West Third at something like three-thirty on a Saturday morning.

"Why, hello," I said. "I certainly want to thank you for helping me out with the song."

"It's a beautiful song," one of them said.

"It's a beautiful evening," I said.

"It was raining earlier."

"Earlier it was the winter of my discontent. Now it's made glorious summer."

"And are we the sons of York?"

"I doubt it," I said, squinting in at them. "You might be the daughters of Lancaster."

"Burt Lancaster? Hey, is Burt Lancaster anybody's father?"

"If we were wise children," another one said, "I suppose we would know."

"Are you a wise child?" another one asked me.

"No, I'm a mad drunken poet."

"Oh, everybody's a mad poet. Are you at least Welsh?"

"My mother came from Ireland," I said. "'Did your mother come from Ireland?'" I sang.

The light had turned green in the course of all this, but the car stayed where it was. Now it turned red again.

"And where did your father come from, mad drunken poet?"

"How would I know? I'm an unwise child."

"Have you a name, mad poet?"

"Mad with a U," I said, "and poet with an E."

"I think I missed that one," somebody said.

"Laurence with a U," I said, making another stab at it. "Clarke with an E."

"Laurence Clarke?"

"Yes, Laurence Clarke the mad poet."

"What do you do when you don't write poems?"

"Everything," I said. "I never write poems. I haven't written a poem for a year and a half."

"Then what do you do?"

I considered this. "I don't edit *Ronald Rabbit's Magazine for Boys and Girls*," I said.

"Neither do I, mad poet."

"Ah, but I did," I said. "Or at least I was presumed to do so, but *Ronald Rabbit's* doesn't exist. I was stowing away on a corporation, and today they fired me."

"Poor mad poet."

The light had turned green again, and the car behind us was using his horn to bring this fact to our attention. "We can't just stand here," one of the girls said.

"We can't drive away," another one said. "We can't leave Mad Poet here. How would we find him again?"

"You mean Laurence Clarke. You shouldn't call him Mad Poet."

"You can call me Mad Poet if you want to."

More honking behind me. The tailgate dropped and the girls in the luggage compartment moved to make room for me. "We'll give Mad Poet a ride," one of them said. "Hop in, Mad Poet. Hop in, M.P."

"Military Police," said a voice from the front.

"No, Member of Parliament. Laurence Clarke, Member of Parliament. Where are you going, Laurence Clarke?"

"To hell in a handcar."

I got inside, and got the tailgate shut behind me. The station wagon lurched forward just as the light turned red. The honker behind us didn't make the signal and went on honking his distress at us as we sped away.

"Where are you going, Mad Poet?"

"Call him Larry. Can we call you Larry? Where are you going, Larry?"

"I don't know."

"Don't you have a home?"

"I don't think so."

"So we'll take him home with us."

"Oh, wouldn't that be brittle!"

"Utterly peanut. Should we kidnap you, Larry?"

"No one would ransom me."

"Then we could keep you forever, and feed you peanut brittle and marmalade."

"And treacle, and weak tea with cream in it."

"How super if we could kidnap him."

"Go ahead," I put in. "Kidnap me. But treacle makes me ill and weak tea with cream in it is very hard to find. I'll have jam tomorrow and jam yesterday, if that's all the same to you."

"Mad Poet knows Alice."

"Mad Poet knew Alice long before you ever fell down any rabbit holes," said Mad Poet. "And Mad Poet feels the same way about little girls that Lewis Carroll did."

"Oh, super! Mad Poet's a dirty old man."

"But not *that* old."

"How old are you, Mad Poet?"

"Thirty-two."

"We're sixteen. Except Naughty Nasty Nancy, who is fifteen."

"A mere child," murmured Naughty Nasty Nancy. She was one of the two in the back seat, and wore a peaked witch's cap and granny glasses.

"Hey, Mad Poet! Where do you want to go?"

"Wherever you're going," I said.

A forest of giggles. "But we're going to Darien!"

"Excellent."

"That's Darien, Connecticut!"

"Only Darien I know," I said.

"Do you really want to come with us?"

"Wherever you want to go," I said, "that's where Mad Poet wants to go. Be it Darien or Delhi or Dubuque. Whither thou goest, Mad Poet shall go. Mad Poet loves you."

"All of us?"

"All of you," I agreed. "Mad Poet loves one and all, including Naughty Nasty Nancy, who is a mere child of fifteen. Mad Poet loves the daughters of Lancaster."

"And the daughters of Lancaster love Mad Poet," said a small voice at my side.

"How nice," said Mad Poet. "How nice indeed."

How nice, friend Steve. How nice indeed to be the Mad Poet, at once disarmingly drunk and brilliantly sober, joyously kidnaped by six winsome refugees from the Convent of the Holy Name. For six little maids from school were they, Steve, six little

32

maids from one of those cloistered mausolea to which the Catholic aristocracy condemn their most nubile daughters for the duration of their delicious adolescences. They had stolen away that night shortly after bed check (bed check!) and had borrowed the car of their algebra teacher. Merry Cat was doing the driving. Merry Cat's name is Mary Katherine O'Shea, and she possesses a license which allows her to drive in the State of Connecticut during daylight hours. If anyone had stopped Merry Cat, she would have been in a whole lot of trouble. No one did, and she wasn't.

Merry Cat is sixteen, as are all of them but Naughty Nasty Nancy, the fifteen-year-old witch-girl whose last name is Hall. Merry Cat does have a feline face, with sharply sloping eyebrows and a quick grin. Her hair is black and her skin very fair, and what she looks like is a very classy Irish girl, which is what she is.

It is also what most of the rest of them are, Irish or Anglo-Irish or Castle Irish or Ascendancy or whatever. Shall I describe the rest of them for you?

All right, I think I will. But only because you insist, Steve-o.

Let's return to the station wagon and do it geographically. Merry Cat, as I said, was driving. Sitting beside her was Dawn Redmond, a soft and quiet girl, soft of face and soft of body, with hair the color of a freshly opened chestnut and a slight complement of freckles on her cheekbones and across the bridge of her nose. She has exceptionally large breasts, and their sensitivity seems to be in proportion to their dimension. She goes all glassy-eyed when they are stroked, and can achieve orgasm from such attention.

In the back seat Naughty Nasty Nancy sat directly behind Dawn. Naughty Nasty Nancy does not speak too often, but her occasional remarks are always incisive. There is a distinctly fey quality to this girl, Steve. If you were casting Hamlet, you would pick her instantly for Ophelia.

On Nancy's right was B.J. B.J. is Barbara Judith Castle. She looks enough like Merry Cat to be her sister, but isn't. They may be cousins. I'm not certain. My memory of the conversation in which that part came up is somewhat vague, and I don't know for certain whether they are cousins or lovers. I'm sure it's one or the other. It's possible, of course, that they are both.

Now for the luggage compartment, where I was sitting in a modified lotus position. On my right, Ellen Jamison, red-haired and slim-hipped and flat-chested and freckled. If her father ever loses his several million dollars, she can always earn a living posing for Norman Rockwell. She even has braces on her teeth.

Let me tell you something, Steve. Nothing brings you all the way back like kissing a girl with braces on her teeth. It makes you want to go home and stand in front of the mirror and squeeze blackheads. An ultimate nostalgia trip as the tongue-tip tickles all that shiny wire.

And on my left, chubby and giggly and bouncy and rosy-cheeked, Alison Keller. She wears her dark-brown hair in a Dutch cut, and her bangs fall upon her unlined brow. She is happy and bubbly and exuberant, and one is so delighted with this side of her that one doesn't suspect there is more. But she paints, does Alison, and I have seen some of her paintings, and they are dark and mordant with echoes of Bosch and Dali, and they are weirdly wonderful, and so is she.

"We are truly kidnaping you, Mad Poet," they kept saying. "And we will keep you hidden away in a cellar and smuggle scraps of food to you from the caf, and every day we will all steal down to you and make mad passionate love to you, and we will never never never let our Mad Poet go."

How nice indeed.

The only hangup on the drive to Darien was that Merry Cat kept bitching about having to drive. "It's not fair," she would say. "Everybody else gets to neck with Mad Poet and all I have is the steering wheel. Doesn't anyone else want to drive?"

No one else had a license. Except Mad Poet, but no one ever had the temerity to suggest that he drive.

"You're always pestering to drive," she accused them, "and now when I'm perfectly willing to let you, nobody wants to all of a sudden."

So I could only neck with five of them, which was a shame. If life were perfect, we would have had a chauffeur. But why carp?

Steve, this was as perfect as life had ever gotten.

Incredible.

You know, I shouldn't have bothered with that geography shtick. It didn't apply for very long. By the time we hit the West Side Drive, Dawn had climbed into the back seat, and she and Nancy and B.J. had done whatever it is you do to the back seats of station wagons to flatten them out, so that the back-seat area just became part of an expanded luggage compartment. So there I was with the five of them, still in this same alcoholic haze and still sober regardless, and I reached out and kissed one, and the little devil opened her mouth instantly, and another one cuddled up and put my hand on her breast, and from there on you can write your own script. I never knew quite whom I was kissing nor whom I was touching at any given time. Nor did it ever quite matter.

The trouble is that I'm making it sound like an orgy, and it wasn't at all like an orgy, not in the least. First of all, there was an air of utter innocence about the proceedings that couldn't have been greater if we had been playing Parcheesi. We all liked each other and we were all having fun and it was all a lazy, giggly, delicious, magical thing.

Absolutely no urgency about it. The kisses were long and deliberate, the petting warm and wholehearted, but there was none of the rise and fall of serious sex about it. I find myself groping for words, perhaps because the whole ambience was one I had never experienced before, neither personally nor in fiction.

How to describe it? I could say that I engaged in two hours of incessant sex play and not only did not have an orgasm, but never much felt like having one. In youth I remember that sort of experience leading to an advanced case of testicular congestion, which I think we used to call Lover's Nuts. I didn't get this now. Perhaps it's because I'm older now, but I rather doubt it.

Oh, hell, most of the time I didn't even have an erection. It is not exactly unheard of for me not to have an erection in erotic situations, as I have not the slightest doubt Fran has told you. (Should you experience similar failings, you're likely to hear about it, man.) But when that happened it was always because my mind was elsewhere, whereas this evening my mind was very much on what was happening. As a matter of fact, I cannot recall ever being so entirely involved in the Now, and entirely concerned with my partners.

So I not only didn't have an erection but I didn't *want* one. I just wanted to go on kissing and fondling and saying clever things and hearing them say clever things. Do you want to know what happened? I fell in love. I fell in love with all five of them. I fell in love with Merry Cat, too, and without laying a hand on her.

We played all the way to Darien, and they said I was their own personal Mad Poet and they would all share me forever, and I told them I wanted to take them all to Utah and marry the six of them and live happily ever after.

"And have children with all of us?"

"Only daughters."

After we go to Darien—

But that's enough. This typewriter not only says what it damned well wants to say, but it knows when it's said enough. I would sort of like to tell you what happened after we got to Darien, and where I spent the night, and what happened the next day, and other things along those lines. I would like to tell you some more about the various girls, and some of the conversations we had and the things we said.

The typewriter has other ideas. It thinks I've said enough, and I have to abide by its decision. That's the way we're doing this.

The girls say they can't understand why Fran left me. That they can't understand why any woman would leave their wonderful Mad Poet. I don't know, Steve, what sort of effect it would have on you if six beautiful, rich, sweet, sixteen-year-old girls said this to you. Maybe you would yawn. Not me. Not bloody likely.

Perhaps I'll write more later. I seem to be in a letter-writing period, and after all, how many people are there for me to write to? So you may be hearing from me again. I might even tell you what happened later on.

Ah, well. It is Monday night and I am in New York, in my humble little flat on Bleecker Street. In a few minutes I will go to sleep in the very same bed where Fran and I so often shared connubial bliss, and in which you and she no doubt shared occasional moments of extranubial bliss. I wonder if I'll dream, and of what.

Send the fifteen hundred as soon as you can, Steve. No big rush, but whenever you can spare it. And keep Fran with you. Not that I have any particular hatred for her, but I don't much want to see her, and I honestly don't think I could fit her into my schedule.

Eat your heart out, you son of a bitch.

Buenos noches,

Larry

MUGGSWORTH, CAULDER, TRAVIS & BEALE
ATTORNEYS-AT-LAW
437 PIPER BOULEVARD
RICHMOND, VIRGINIA 23219

17 June

Mr. Laurence Clarke
74 Bleecker Street
New York, New York 10012

Dear Mr. Clarke:

I am writing to you on behalf of our client Mrs. Lisa Clarke, in reference to her telephone conversation with you on 12 June and your letter to her of that date.

As of today's date, your alimony payment to our client is seventeen (17) days overdue. While the special circumstances described in both your telephone conversation and your letter might ordinarily be construed as mitigating, your previous history of incessant delinquency in rendering such monies to Mrs. Clarke leads inevitably to the assumption that the present delinquency is nothing more than adherence to a standard pattern. In light of the above, I can only urge that you make speedy payment in the amount of eight hundred fifty dollars ($850) in lawful money to my client, and must advise you that unless such payment reaches this office within one (1) week we will have no course open but to seek legal redress.

Furthermore, I must insist on Mrs. Clarke's behalf that you cease and desist from entering into any communications with her of the order of your most recent letter of 12 June. As you perhaps recall, the terms of your separation agreement with Mrs. Clarke, later embodied in your agreement of divorce, forbade any such unwarranted communication on the part of either party. Mrs. Clarke does not welcome such verbal attention from you, nor does she have the slightest wish to be made privy to aspects of your life as discussed in the aforementioned communication. It is our considered opinion that such communication constitutes a direct and unwarranted invasion of privacy, and a repetition of the offense will be dealt with accordingly.

I might further take it upon myself to state that both the tone and nature of the communication above described is such as to raise serious questions as to your own mental and emotional state. In this connection, let me offer the disinterested suggestion that you seriously contemplate seeking responsible psychiatric guidance, should you be financially capable of so doing after having discharged your just obligations to Mrs. Clarke.

I remain, sir, your most obedient servant,

Roland David Caulder

RDC:sj

74 Bleecker St.
New York 10012
June 19

Mr. Roland David Caulder
Muggsworth, Caulder, Travis & Beale
437 Piper Blvd.
Richmond, Va.

Dear Mr. Caulder:

I cannot thank you sufficiently for your letter of 17 June on behalf of your client Mrs. Lisa Clarke. It is entirely possible that I will have it framed.

It shames me to admit that of which you no doubt have by now apprised yourself, to wit, that there is no check for eight hundred fifty dollars ($850) in this envelope. My ability to discharge my just obligation to your client is contingent upon the success of a new business venture presently in the formative stages. While the details are necessarily cloaked in secrecy at present, I suppose I can tell you at least that my associates and I are planning a coast-to-coast network of blood banks. Rather than depend upon human volunteers, we intend to use turnips.

Let me thank you as well for your expressions of concern over my mental and emotional health. I too have had my doubts on that score, and have been pondering the entire problem for the past two or three hours (2-3 hrs.). As I cannot presently see my way clear to employing professional help in this regard, I wonder if I might impose upon you to apply your esteemed diagnostic talents to another letter. Toward this end, I am taking the liberty of enclosing a Xerox copy of my letter of fifteen June (15/6) to Mr. Stephen Joel Adel. You may remember that Mr. Adel was mentioned in the earlier communication previously cited.

I look forward with interest to your reply.

Very truly yours,

Laurence Clarke

74 Bleecker St.
New York 10012
June 19

Mrs. Lisa Clarke
219 Maple Rd.
Richmond, Va.

Dear Lisa:

Christ, have they been spiking your father's Ken-L-Ration lately? You wouldn't believe the letter I got from the old bastard. I'm enclosing a Xerox copy of it along with my reply. You'll note I sent him a copy of my letter to Steve. See if you can get him to show it to you. I know he won't want to, and I also know it's unethical of him to withhold it. I'd be interested to know which way the son of a bitch jumps.

Has he gotten worse lately or what? He's always been pretty bad, but that letter was the limit. I mean, has he reached the point where he talks like that around the house?

Must end this, fun though it is. Jennifer's in the shower, and I have to get her dressed and out of here before the girls get down from Darien.

But before I go, I want to say that you've got to stop bugging me about the money. I might send it if I had it (though I'm not sure I would, to tell you the truth) but I don't have it, and won't have it in the foreseeable future, so you and the old bastard have got to call it quits for the time being. I really think you ought to marry Wally. But you'd better elope with him. If he meets your father before the wedding, there goes the wedding.

Be assured that I have only my own best interests at heart.

Passionately,

Mad Poet

WHITESTONE PUBLICATIONS, INC.
67 West 44th Street
New York 10036

From the desk of Clayton Finch, President

June 18

Mr. Laurence Clarke
74 Bleecker Street
New York 10012

Dear Mr. Clarke:

This is to advise you that a check of our records indicates that our terminal payment to you included an improper over-payment of $75.63. We would appreciate your remitting payment in that amount at your earliest possible convenience.

We also understand that you have on several occasions since leaving Whitestone's employ returned to our offices to avail yourself of the Xerox machine. Mr. Finch has asked me to remind you that use of the Xerox facility is restricted to company business. While it is true that employees of Whitestone habitually disregard this corporate policy, Mr. Finch feels it is ridiculous in the extreme to extend such latitude to those who are no longer with us.

Your attention to this matter will be appreciated.

Sincerely,

Rozanne Gumbino
Secretary to Mr. Finch

RG/s

LAURENCE CLARKE, EDITOR
June 19

Miss Rozanne Gumbino
Whitestone Publications, Inc.
67 West 44th St.
New York 10036

Dear Rozanne:

Thanks very much for your letter. I've been getting quite a few letters lately, and I've been writing more letters myself than is my usual custom, but I wanted to take the time to let you know that your letter was one of my favorites. On the off chance that you failed to keep a carbon of it, I'm enclosing herewith a Xerox copy for your files.

As far as your overpayment to me of $75.63 is concerned, I can only suggest that you contact my attorney. I am sure he will assist in sorting this matter out and seeing it through to a mutually satisfactory solution. He is Roland Davis Caulder of Muggsworth, Caulder, Travis & Beale, with offices at 437 Piper Boulevard in Richmond, Virginia.

It certainly is good hearing from you, Rozanne. At the risk of offending you, I must admit that I barely remember you, having only had contact with you on the day I severed my connection with Whitestone. I remember your voice on the telephone, rather low-pitched and throbby, and I seem to recall that you have big tits.

Why don't you come down to Bleecker Street and I'll eat your box.

Sincerely yourself,

Laurence Clarke
Editor (Ret.)

Dear Larry—

I promised Fran I wouldn't write to you. But she went down to the market to shop for dinner and there are a couple of things I wanted to say.

I'm glad you're taking this well. I don't suppose I have to tell you that we certainly didn't plan for everything to happen at once this way. I mean your losing your job the same day you lost Fran. Although if you think about it, Larry, you lost Fran a long time before the 12th of June. And I'm not talking about when she and I first fell in love, either. Your marriage went sour, Larry, and after that it was just a question of time before someone stepped in. You know that yourself.

Believe me, I didn't want to be the one. I resisted it for a long time, as a matter of fact. But there was always this very strong current of attraction existing between Frances and myself, not merely a physical thing but emotional as well. If you'll forgive me for pointing it out, Fran and I were always closer in this respect than were she and you. Even long before there was anything between us in any sense. It was just the way we responded to one another, a matter of human rapport.

Then one day we just sort of looked at each other and something happened. It's that kind of situation where the words in the stupid pop tunes all seem to not only make sense but to have a private and personal message just for the two of us. As your friend—and I still consider myself your friend, and hope you consider me that way too, well—as your friend I can wish you nothing more than that you yourself find this kind of love someday with somebody, perhaps somebody you've always known, perhaps someone you have not even met yet.

Larry, as far as the fifteen hundred is concerned, Frances feels that it's her fair share of what the two of you owned in common. In other words, not to cloud this up with any legal bullshit, she says you can keep all the furniture and kitchen utensils and odds and ends, and in return she'll keep the money she took out of the checking account. If you want to be technical, it came to a little less than fifteen hundred. Frances has the exact figure, which I think ran somewhere in the neighborhood of $1475 or $1480.

The point is that on the one hand you don't have to worry about me sending Frances back to you, since no power on earth could make me give up what the two of us have together, but I guess you can't count on me sending the $1500 either, I mean the $1475, because in the first place I don't have it and in the second Fran says it's rightfully hers, and I have to go along with her on that.

Another thing I have to mention is the letter you sent me, which I got in Cuernavaca. Of course I showed it to Fran, although I can't honestly say it was something I wanted to show her. But in the kind of relationship the two of us have, well, we just don't keep secrets from one another, not even in small matters and certainly not in big ones, and so I showed it to her.

She found it a little unsettling, and speaking frankly, old buddy, so did I. My first reaction, actually, was that I was glad you were taking everything almost too well. But on second reading, or what you might call reading between the lines, I found myself changing my mind. For one thing I sensed a very definite undercurrent of hostility throughout the letter, and without going into a lot of Freudian bullshit I would be less worried if the hostility were right out there in the open than the way it is in your letter, sort of hiding behind the bushes and lurking.

And that whole fantasy about the teen-age girls. To tell you the truth, I did think it was amusing and imaginative on your part to invent that routine, but Frances made me realize that it was also pretty sick, and I do mean sick. According to her, you always had a tendency to live a fantasy life that was more real to you than your real life. I would not go that far, although I always felt you may have had your feet planted a little less firmly on the ground than some of the rest of us. I always just figured that this was part of being a poet, the sensitivity bit.

But Fran says that it's almost as if you actually believe the bit with the girls from the convent school. I didn't think that was possible but on rereading the section, I have to agree with her. If that's the case, or whatever's the case, maybe you're wasting your talents as a poet, fella. Maybe you ought to write dirty books or something.

Just kidding, as I'm sure you know.

But what I'm getting at, Larry, in my usual round-about way, is that I hope you won't write any letters of that sort to us again. I don't mean that we are not interested in you and don't want to know how things are going with you, because we are and we do.

That letter, though, was very upsetting to Fran, and to me too. The remarks you made about your private life with Fran and other things like that are not the sort of thing that belong in a letter, and if the purpose was to drive a wedge between the two of us, although I don't honestly think you had that idea in mind, to give you the benefit of the doubt, well, if that was your purpose I have to tell you it pretty much fell flat on its face.

I'm a pretty straightforward guy, as you well know, and I prefer to take your whole letter and everything else pretty much at face value as an honest attempt to let me know, and Fran in the bargain, that you're not holding a grudge. So I'll think of the letter that way whether that's what you had in mind or not.

Anyway, please, no more letters like that. And if you do write, don't refer to this letter, as I don't intend to tell Fran I wrote to you.

Your friend,

Steve

Mrs. Laurence Clarke
c/o American Express
Cuernavaca, Mexico

Dear Fran:

I have a lot of things to tell you, but perhaps the first and most important is what great good fortune you've had to run off with a man who really loves you. I know Steve has always had a problem in communicating, although God knows he's not as hopeless in conversation as he is when he takes pen in hand and tries to write something. But I have a feeling that he may not have let you know fully how he feels about you, and communication is such a problem among lovers, as you can certainly appreciate.

So for that reason I'm taking the liberty of enclosing herewith (if you'll pardon the formal language) a Xerox copy of a letter I received from him. It's handwritten, but I'm happy to say the writing reproduced nicely. That Xerox machine is a really wonderful thing. I've had some correspondence which indicates I may find it increasingly difficult to gain access to it. I hope this will all work out, however.

To return to Steve's letter, you'll notice that it doesn't bear any date. I doubt this will make much difference to you, but at the moment I'm rather involved with correspondence in general, rather compulsive about the whole subject, as it happens, and it would make my record-keeping more complete if you could find out just when it was written and relay the information to me.

It should be easy for you to work it out, actually. As you'll note from an examination of its contents, Steve's letter was written while you were out shopping for something to cook for dinner. Since cooking dinner has never been something you do more than once or twice a week, I'm sure you can narrow things down and work out the timing for me. God knows I would appreciate it.

I want you to really read Steve's letter, Fran. And try not to be put off by the man's relative clumsiness with the English language. After all, he's a photographer and not a writer, and you don't expect photographers to be up to their asses in verbal facility. They're far more apt to be up to their asses in darkroom chemicals, aren't they? Besides, as everyone learns at a tender age, a picture is worth a thousand words. You might say that Steve sent me a picture, as his letter runs quite close to a thousand words. Do you suppose it's just coincidence?

You can tell from a glance at this primitive word-picture of Steve's that he really loves you, Fran. (Somehow I can't bring myself to call you Frances, although Steve seems to refer to you that way a lot. Is it his idea of a pet name?) His love for you is evident in every split infinitive, in every mawkish turn of phrase. In fact I would go so far as to say that his letter to me was in fact a letter to you, a letter he lacked the self-confidence and, oh, the slick glibness to deliver to you in person. And so he writes his letter to you but addresses and mails it to me.

I can understand this, actually. I've been writing all these letters to various people lately and can't entirely dismiss the nagging suspicion that I'm really writing them to myself. Or that my typewriter is writing them to me. I've tended to anthropomorphize my typewriter lately. This may be bad, but I feel it's better than ignoring it.

Thus my passing this letter on to you is in a sense my method of playing the John Alden part, but this is one John Alden who will respectfully decline to speak for himself.

One interesting reason for assuming Steve's letter was written for your benefit, Fran, is his stubborn insistence upon going to such great lengths to suggest that the whole bit with the convent girls never happened. That it was all some fantasy of mine, which I wrote to him for some nefarious purpose. Steve has known me a long time, longer than almost anyone, and he can certainly tell when I'm telling the truth, so he knows dammed well that this happened. I may have had to reconstruct some of the conversation slightly, but I wouldn't be surprised if it came within a couple of words of being a verbatim transcript of what actually went down that night. I guess he must feel that my boasting—and let's admit it, I *was* boasting—reflected somehow on your femininity, as if I were not only doing a rooster strut but also comparing you adversely to the six girls.

A strut, yes; an adverse comparison, surely not. Of course we both know, we all three know, that you are a few years more than sixteen, Fran(ces), and that you will not be sixteen again unless science does something phenomenal. And while twenty-nine is also a hell of a good age, asserted by most authorities to be a woman's sexual peak, there's no gainsaying the fact that after a certain point in life the bloom begins to leave the rose, as the poets say. But question your femininity? Christ, I would never dream of doing that. Quite the opposite. Why, if memory serves, in that very letter I devoted quite a bit of space to unequivocal praise of your oral abilities.

But just to make things as clear as possible, to make things Presidentially clear, as it were, perhaps I'd better tell you a little bit more about the Darien business.

First off, when we got to Darien, nothing happened. (Now if this were a fantasy, something damn well would have happened. To put it another way, if I were allowed to write the script for my life, I'd smooth out a lot of the wrinkles.) But by the time the station wagon got us where we were going, it was somewhere around five or five-thirty and I had a headache and the girls were exhausted. Besides, they had to be in bed so that the nun who was in charge of their dormitory could wake them at seven-thirty. They had managed to sneak out after bed check, and now they had to sneak in before reveille.

I wasn't too thrilled about this, actually. They took me to a squat red-brick building in town and led me up a flight of stairs to a faintly furnished room and told me I could sleep there.

"Who lives here?" I wondered.

"No one."

"It's only eight dollars a week, Larry, and we six chip in to pay the rent. It's secret, you might say."

"It's refuge from the storm, you might say."

"It's a safe place to fuck, you might even say."

"Ah," I said, nodding thoughtfully. I walked over to the bed and bounced on it. "A good bed," I said.

"Well used."

"And there's just room for the seven of us," I said.

"Oh, we can't stay."

"Can a couple of you stay?"

"Not a chance."

"God on a pogo stick, can at least one of you stay?"

"No way."

"It hardly seems fair," said Mad Poet.

They explained the situation, and fair or not it seemed to be The Way Things Were. They all assured me of their undying love and lust, and I necked them each good-bye in turn, and they went away and I went to sleep.

Passed out, actually. But neatly, after having first removed my clothes and hung them ever so neatly in a corner of the floor. And then I popped into that snug double bed and pulled up the covers and slept.

I hadn't really thought I would be able to manage this last. I don't honestly think I would have had the strength to fuck anybody just then, but the last thing I wanted was to have to sleep alone. I never much liked sleeping alone, and I particularly dreaded it that night. Exhaustion and India Pale Ale have a way of conquering that form of dread, though, and I went out like a burned-out bulb.

I awoke very abruptly. There was this shadowy dream that I do not remember, and then I was completely awake and complete aware of a presence curled up behind me. I was sleeping on my side, body curled in a semifetal posture, and a body was similarly curled behind me. A very soft and warm body. I felt soft thighs cushioning my buttocks and firm breasts pressing into my back, and while I was trying to decide whether or not to let on that I was awake, a small hand came around my shoulder and fastened itself over my eyes.

"Guess who," a voice demanded.

"Victory McLaglen. Do another."

A giggle. "Do you even know where you are?"

"I seem to have gone to heaven," I said. "The funny thing is that I don't remember dying."

"Aren't you going to guess? Or don't you honestly remember?"

"Ah, I remember. I remember everything. I have to guess which one you are, eh?"

"Uh-huh."

"What happens if I guess right?"

"Then we can make love."

"What if I guess wrong?"

"We still make love but I won't enjoy it as much. And I'm sure you want me to enjoy it."

"Merry Cat," I said.

She squealed and took her hand away, and I turned around and looked into her cat's eyes and kissed her little mouth. Her face was flushed.

"Oh God," she said. "Oh, you're ready, Oh, how nice. Don't wait, don't even touch me, just get in me. I want you inside me, I can't wait."

She wasn't exaggerating. She got off the minute I was inside her, coming in a sweet soft pink dissolve. She came twice more and then it was my turn, and then we clung to each other while I waited for the earth tremors to quit shaking hell out of the room.

Ultimately she said, "How on earth did you guess right? Just a shot in the dark?"

"Not exactly that."

"An intuitive flash? You just felt it suddenly in your heart and soul?"

"I felt things in quite a few places, but that's not it."

"You recognized my voice, then."

"Well, no."

"No? Hmmm. Uh, let's see, uh, you could feel my breasts against you and you figured it was me by process of elimination because they were the only ones you weren't familiar with."

"Wrong again."

"I think I give up."

"Just logic," I said. "You had to drive last night and you didn't have a chance to come in back, so for the sake of fairness they let

51

you come over this morning. That's how I figured it out, and it looks as though I was right."

"Oh," she said.

"What's the matter?"

"Well, nothing, actually. And, see, that was exactly what I told them this morning, the five of them. Just that very line of reasoning. '*You five had Mad Poet all to yourselves last night and now it should be my turn.*'"

"That's just what I just said."

"Right, and it's what I said, and I thought it was totally brittle, and they wouldn't buy it. Instead we all cut cards and I won."

"Oh."

"That's really weird, working it all out logically like that and being wrong and coming up with the right answer. It's pretty far out."

"Well, even on a straight guess I had one chance in six."

"True."

I started saying something, God knows what, and she reached out her little hand again, only this time instead of putting it over my eyes, she wrapped it around my cock. Whatever I was saying seemed no longer relevant. I reached out with both hands and began playing with her.

"They'll be coming over fairly soon."

"Here?"

She nodded, started to say something, then gasped when I touched one of the right buttons. I slipped a finger inside her. She was sopping wet and hot enough to cook an egg on and unbelievably tight.

(That's another advantage in being sixteen, Fran, and if Steve thinks that my mentioning it is any sort of implicit criticism of you, he's out of his skull. It's a simple biological fact. Certain organs do lose a certain portion of their elasticity over the years. But that's not to suggest that you have to start worrying about men falling out of you, or about your being unable to tell for sure whether they're in there or not. You've got quite a few years to go before that'll become a problem for you, and by then sex will be so much less frequent an indulgence, and so less important to you, that you won't really be giving up all that much.)

Where was I? Oh, yes. 'She was sopping wet and hot enough to cook an egg on and unbelievably tight.' That's where I was.

I said, "We have time to do it again, don't we?"

"Sure."

"But let's not rush this one."

"No, let's not."

"Because I'd like to get very well acquainted with your body. So that I won't have to guess whether or not it's you I'm in bed with."

"Slow is better," she said.

"Usually."

"Only last time I couldn't wait."

"I understand."

"I think you have the most beautiful cock in the world, Larry."

The rest of the girls came just after we did, happily enough. (I mean that it was happy they waited until we were through, not that we came happily. Although we did, but it would have been a more awkward construction that way. I'm pointing this out primarily for Steve's benefit, Fran, so that he can learn to develop more of an ear for narrative. If he's going to insist on sending me a thousand words when a simple photograph would suffice, it would be best if he learned to arrange them in the proper order.)

They came like Greeks, bringing me little presents. While none of their gifts matched what Merry Cat had brought me, I was grateful for the two containers of cardboard coffee, the grilled-cheese-and-bacon sandwich, the socks and underwear.

"I couldn't remember whether you wore jockey shorts or boxer shorts," Alison said, blue eyes sparkling and plump cheeks glowing. "But Naughty Nasty Nancy remembered."

"Hardly the sort of thing she'd forget," B.J. said.

"Meow," said Nancy Hall. She was still wearing the witch's hat, and mordant madness danced in her eyes. "Meow, meow, meow. Look at Merry Cat, she's positively radiant. Orgasm brings the most beatific look to her face. Are you in a state of grace, Marry Katherine?"

"Sure, and don't I half feel sinfully saintlike," Merry Cat said.

"Sister Theresa talks like that. Do her some more, Merry Cat."

"Faith, and am I not a fair candidate for canonization, with the Spirit of the Holy Name running down my leg."

"I think that's blasphemous," Dawn Redmond said.

"Sure and you're nothing but jealous, Dawn me love."

"Oh, shut up and kiss me, Merry Cat," Dawn said.

They kissed and went into a clinch. Merry Cat and I had our clothes on again. The rest of the girls and I were sitting on the bed or leaning against the wall, and Dawn and Merry Cat were standing up in the middle of the room with their arms around each other and their tongues in each other's mouth. We all watched for a while, and Naughty Nasty Nancy kissed B.J. on the neck and touched her breasts, and Alison petted Naughty Nasty Nancy gently on the bottom, and Ellen Jamison cuddled beside me on the bed and opened her mouth so wide for my kiss that the braces didn't get in the way. And eventually Dawn and Merry Cat let go of each other, and they both had a glassy look in their eyes, and Dawn said, "Well, at least Larry hasn't spoiled you for me, Merry Cat. I guess I still can turn you on."

"Till the day I die, Dawn."

"Isn't it nice," said Ellen to me, "that we all love each other so truly?"

There's not really much to add to this. It's not as if I felt compelled to burden you with a blow-by-blow description of my life without you, anyway. I just wanted to put you in the picture, so to speak, and it seems to have taken me several thousand words to do it.

That's a really terrible school, incidentally. They have all of these seventeenth-century rules administered by a batch of desiccated nuns who spend most of their time remembering the good old days with Torquemada. My six little daughters of Lancaster seem to be the six really fine girls in the school. As B.J. put it, "We're really alone here. Nobody else drinks and nobody else smokes and nobody else turns on and nobody else fucks. There are some lesbians, but they're hopeless. All so sickeningly sincere about it. When they're not eating each other, they're praying over it. You could really vomit, honestly."

Fortunately, these six have parental permission to sign out for overnights with mythical New York aunts and uncles. That afternoon B.J. and Alison signed out, and Merry Cat drove us to the station, and we rode into Grand Central on the New Haven. We just kept talking about things. Total rapport. I can understand how exciting it must be for you and Steve. There was a phrase in his letter about the words in popular songs being endowed with personal meaning when you're in love. I haven't put it as well as he did, of course, but I know what he means. I wouldn't say that I was getting any secret flashes out of the transistor radio a few seats down the aisle, but it was that sort of very vital feeling you get when you interact in utter honest intimacy with another human being, or, in this case, with two other human beings.

We talked about you, Fran, but I didn't tell them anything you wouldn't want them to know. Set your mind at ease.

There was an odd moment just as the train left Westport when the two girls exchanged a brief but thorough soul-kiss right there in front of everybody. You could hear the jaws fall. But nonembarrassment is as contagious as embarrassment, and the girls were totally cool about it, and so was I. I wish Steve had been around to take pictures of the faces of some of the other passengers.

Then we got to New York and I took them over to the Feenjon for dinner, and we listened to music for a while, and then we all went back to the apartment and balled.

Dawn came in the following week, which is to say, this past Saturday. I thought she would be bringing one of the other girls along too, but nobody else could get away. It's exam week, or exam week is coming up, or something. They're all in the same class, with another year to go before they graduate. I guess school will let out this week or next, and not all of them will be spending the summer in the New York area, but they have solemnly assured me that I will have balled all six of them before they leave for wherever they're going. There are only two that I haven't gotten to so far, Ellen and Nancy. I wouldn't want to miss out on either of them, believe me.

I didn't know if I would be able to handle Dawn. If I'd be up to it, that it. Oh, you know what I mean. Because I spent the previous night with Jennifer and was slightly exhausted. Smoked a lot of grass, and while it had more or less worn off I still felt faintly spaced out. I was relieved when just one of them showed up, and relieved too that it was Dawn, because all anyone had to do to please her was pay proper attention to her breasts, and anyone who wouldn't want to do that would have to have something the matter with his head.

Anyway, I surprised myself. It was really a sensational evening, and I use the term advisedly.

So here it is, Monday, and I keep telling myself that I ought to go out and look for a job, and I think I might have done just that, except I got this letter from Steve and wanted to answer it right away. Although I don't suppose you would say that I am answering his letter, Fran(ces), since it's you I'm writing to. But in the sense of this letter being in response to the other letter, then I guess it constitutes an answer.

A few paragraphs ago I was going to say that being in bed with two girls at once reminded me of the conversation with Bill Adams, but I don't think I sent you that conversation. Unless I'm mistaken, that was in a letter I wrote to Lisa. I'll allude to it anyway, Fran, on the chance that you might see a copy of that letter sometime, or that you might have an affair with Lisa yourself, as far as that goes. Did you ever have anything going with another girl? You always swore you didn't, but that might have been because you thought I wouldn't approve of something. Now that it no longer matters whether or not I approve of what you do or have done, I wish you would answer that question again. I'd be damned interested. An honest answer would probably explain a lot about you. Of course there's no reason why you should have to explain aspects of yourself to me, but I would be interested.

Please keep in touch.

Love,

Pancho Villa

P.S.: It occurs to me that I haven't said anything about the fifteen hundred dollars which seems to have shrunk to $1480, and which also seems to have turned from our money into your money. You managed to figure out that the whole thing ought to belong to you, on the theory that you were leaving me our ratty furniture and the unwashed dishes and some of your dirty underwear. (Or did you want me to send the underwear along? I'd be glad to, but I don't know if they would allow me to send it through the mail, let alone across international boundaries. But just say the word and I'll look into the situation more closely. If you don't want them, I can probably sell the lot to one of those funky-underwear freaks.)

I can see your point, Fran, but I'm afraid you're not seeing things in their true perspective. Love can do this, and I think the air of total illogic which you share with Steve is proof enough of the bond of devotion that unites you. But let me try to bring things more clearly into focus for you.

Like you, I started with the premise that the $1480 (if you insist) was in the nature of community property, belonging equally to both of us. While it's true that I was the one who put most of the money in the account, you were the one who barely managed not to spend all of it, so I guess that makes us equal partners in the venture.

I figure we're also equal partners in the debts that existed when you walked out, and they came to a great deal more than the balance in the account, especially when one includes the money I owe Lisa, which after all must be included since I owed it to her before you decided to dissolve the partnership and merge your shares with Stevie Boy. In that sense, if you follow this through all the way, you owe me more than $1480. You owe me a lot more like two grand, but I've decided to call it even at $1480 by pretending that our furniture is worth $520.

And no matter how deeply you and Steve are in love, you still can't be misty-eyed enough to believe that the crap in our apartment is worth anywhere near that much. If the sagging bed and the leaking sofa and all that garbage are worth $520, then the Salvation Army store on Thompson Street has assets greater than General Motors. Let's face facts, honey. I would have to pay someone to haul this *dreck* out of here. If I stuck it out on the sidewalk, everybody would walk right past it.

You owe me money, Fran(ces). We both know this, and at least one of us knows that sooner or later you are going to make it good.

I have faith in you.

P.V.

From the desk of Clayton Finch, President

June 22

Mr. Laurence Clarke
74 Bleecker Street
New York 10012

Dear Mr. Clarke:

You may recall that I once described you as having stowed away on a corporation. It would now appear that you are attempting to hang onto the hull of Whitestone Publications, Inc., with the tenacity of a barnacle. It is my sad duty to pry you loose and cast you adrift, hoping that you will escape the waves of poverty and reach the shores of gainful employment.

For some reason you seem disinclined to return our unintentional overpayment in the amount of $75.63. While I find your attitude deplorable, I cannot deny that I find it equally unsurprising. On the chance that your affairs were in litigation of some sort, I did direct a brief letter in this regard to the attorney you mentioned in your letter to my secretary. He replied over the telephone and I must admit I was quite incapable of making out what he was getting at. Either you are up to one of your intricate little pranks or you are desperately in need of a better-qualified legal counselor. The man was either terribly confused or a raving maniac.

But the overpayment is minor. While our legal staff would no doubt caution me against saying as much, we would be heartily glad to forget the $75.63 if it were equally possible to forget you in the bargain.

I refer, of course, to your continued unauthorized use of our Xerox machine.

You might be astonished, Mr. Clarke, to know quite how many memoranda your conduct has inspired. The most annoying aspect of all about your behavior is that you seem inclined to make an extra copy of everything you Xerox, which you then leave in the vicinity of the machine. These bits of *Kilroy Was Here* nonsense have been passed around several offices, particularly in the sales and editorial departments, and have occasioned slight amusement in certain quarters and considerable embarrassment for certain other parties. They also constitute a thorn in the side of the personnel responsible for supervising the Xerox machine. It would seem that you are to them as Robin Hood was to the Sheriff of Nottingham. Any number of traps have been laid for you, Mr. Clarke, but you seem to walk right through them. The situation is further complicated by the fact that no one seems to remember what you look like, due to the reclusive nature of your stay here and the lack of interaction between you and other employees. While your features are ineradicably engraved upon my own memory, I have better things to do than stand around all day watching the Xerox machine.

As you can no doubt appreciate, I am not able to view all of this without a certain degree of humor. My sense of humor is your life preserver, Mr. Clarke. A more humorless man would no doubt have you arrested.

I, on the other hand, merely wish to issue an order. At no time are you to make use of the Whitestone Publication, Inc., Xerox machine. At no time are you to enter the premises of Whitestone Publications, Inc. At no time are you to utilize any Whitestone letterhead, or to in any way identify yourself as editor of *Ronald Rabbit's Magazine for Boys and Girls.*

Nor are you at any time to direct any obscene and insulting communications to my secretary, or any communications, obscene or otherwise, to me.

Yours very truly,

Clayton Finch

CF/rg

Ronald Rabbit's Magazine for Boys and Girls
67 West 44th Street
New York 10036

LAURENCE CLARKE, EDITOR

June 23

Mr. Clayton Finch, Pres.
Whitestone Publications, Inc.
67 West 44th St.
New York 10036

Dear Mr. Finch:

First of all, let me say that I hope you have no objections to my making use of my remaining stock of *Ronald Rabbit's* stationery. I took it along only because you suggested that I clean out my desk, and a stack of letterheads and envelopes was all I could find. I felt that the letterhead of a defunct magazine bearing the name of an editor no longer in your employ would be of small use to anyone at Whitestone. I know that such material is occasionally put to use as scrap paper. It seemed to me at the time, however, that Whitestone was in little danger of a scrap-paper shortage, what with the constant stream of executives seeking new employment and the sad parade of magazines and whole divisions folding up and vanishing into limbo.

In any case, I resolved at the time to use the *Ronald Rabbit's* letterhead only for correspondence directly relating to the welfare of Whitestone. While I am no longer a member of the Whitestone crew, I still cannot help feeling a vested interest in the ship's sailing a clearly charted course.

It is in this spirit that this present letter is offered, and I can only hope that it will prove valuable, to everyone from yourself as Captain of the Ship down to the lowliest member of the crew, and indeed to the whole entity that *is* Whitestone.

I have several suggestions, so let me take them one at a time:

(1) It seems to me that, while an incident well known to both of us (and to half the world) may have been responsible for the commercial failure of *Ronald Rabbit's,* the magazine may have had a strike against it to begin with. I refer, of course, to the charge of male chauvinism which was ofttimes leveled at us. Could we not revive the magazine, in essentially the same format—though slightly updated, needless to say—but with a change of title? Reborn as *Rachel Rabbit's Magazine for Girls and Boys*, it would seem that we would be *au courant* in a rather exciting way. I had first considered the title *Rozanne Rabbit's Magazine for Girls and Boys* but rejected it for the time being on the grounds that it might provoke any number of "inside gags" in the publishing industry concerning an executive secretary with that first name who is possessed, if you will, of an insatiable appetite for carrots. This would not be a problem with Rachel, or, come to think of it, with Rosalie, Rhonda, Ruth or Rita.

(2) Should your reaction to (1) be favorable, I would beg to be considered for the post of editor. I should be glad to submit a résumé upon request, and, if policy dictates, would willingly assume the *nom de guerre* of Laura Clarke for the term of employment.

(3) This last point may well be the most important of all. In any mammoth corporation, Mr. Finch, an executive is faced with the problem of delegating authority wisely. One cannot take too much upon one's own shoulders, nor yet can one put too much trust in the good judgment of inferiors.

What brings this all home is a letter I today received. It seems to have originated from your office, and was either signed by a subordinate or, in the crush of daily work, was signed by yourself without you having taken the time to read it. A glance will assure you that you would not at your worst moment be capable of producing such drivel. While a letter of this sort directed to me would have no obvious repercussions, you can surely imagine the results if a more important letter were handled in this fashion. For that matter, even this particular letter could have unfortunate results should it be widely circulated among, for example, editorial and sales personnel. While the work *laughing-stock* is a bit strong, I'm sure the point is clear to you.

In the event that you do not have a copy of the letter at hand, I am enclosing herewith a Xerox copy for your attention.

With all good wishes,

Laurence Clarke
Editor Emeritus

LC/s
Enc.

LAURENCE CLARKE, EDITOR

June 23

Miss Rozanne Gumbino
Whitestone Publication, Inc.
67 West 44th Street
New York 10036

Dearest Rozanne:

The offer still holds, you gorgeous cunt, you.

Hungrily,

The Phantom

74 Bleecker St.
New York 10012
June 23

Mr. Ronald David Caulder, Esq.
Muggsworth, Caulder, Travis & Beale
437 Piper Blvd.
Richmond, Va.

Dear Mr. Caulder:

I have it on reasonably good authority that you are presently engaged in the preparation of a suit of defamation of character against Mr. Clayton Finch, President of Whitestone Publications, Inc.

This puts me in a rather awkward position, as I have ties of allegiance to both Mr. Finch and yourself, having served one in the capacity of editor and the other in the capacity of son-in-law. My first impulse was to sit this one out on the sidelines, but further reflection has convinced me that neutrality in this instance would be cowardly and irresponsible.

Accordingly, I'm enclosing herewith a Xerox copy of a letter I received today from Mr. Finch. You'll note his reference to yourself in the passage I've marked. His characterization of you as "either terribly confused or a raving maniac," and his recommendation that I cease to employ you professionally, would certainly seem to be actionable. Of course mine is only a lay opinion in every sense of the word, and you will no doubt be better able to judge this point.

At the same time, I do owe a measure of loyalty to Mr. Finch for past favors. Thus, should this matter ever come to court, it would be my duty to testify on his behalf. I would then confirm his charge and would testify that, during the time I have know you, you have frequently been terribly confused and have more than occasionally acted the role of a raving maniac.

My regards to your client Mrs. Clarke. Please convey to her my best wishes for success in her forthcoming marriage.

Very truly yours,

Laurence Clarke

LC/s
Enc.

Dear Larry,

I ought to know better than to write you this letter. You'll probably send a copy of it to my father, or to *The New York Times,* or God only knows where. And I get the feeling that the more I ask you not to, the more likely it is that you will, which gives me pause. I've always said that you were the strangest person I've ever known. That's your charm, sugar loaf, but it's also your downfall. I think right now your madness has taken its strangest form to date. I've heard of dancing manias and praying manias. There was a poet, Christopher Smart, who used to make his friends fall down in the streets of London and pray with him. They tucked him away in Bedlam. Samuel Johnson said he didn't think the man was all that mad, and that he'd as soon fall down and pray in the streets with Kit Smart as anyone else in London.

Why am I telling you this? I think it's because there's nobody to talk to about anything much more complex than the weather and baseball. Dammit, I miss New York. It's nice breathing fresh air, but it gives you all this energy, lover, and then you have nothing to do with it because you're in Richmond. Or rather I'm in Richmond.

But to get back to you. You seem to have a correspondence mania, and I don't understand it, but I can see where it might be fun. And at least you're writing something. You know, sometimes I think that's why I left you. You were a writer and you weren't writing anything, and that went against the grain of the old Protestant Ethic, of which I suppose I'm still a willing captive.

Hmmmm. Why, indeed, am I telling you this? I guess to warn you to be careful of Father. You know about his bark. His bite is even worse. Please do not provoke him.

You're going to send him this fucking letter. I just know you are. Dammit, don't.

Well, Richmond is beginning to get to me, as I think I said. I'm getting the old urge for a trip to Big Town. Thought I might come up next weekend and take in a couple of shows. Maybe I'll give you a ring and we can gripe about old times or something.

If I thought you could be trusted, I would make you a deal. I know you can't, but I'll offer the deal anyway. If you'll quit mailing things to Daddy, especially this letter, I'll stop trying to get blood from your turnip. In other words, I'll lay off on the alimony demands until you start to get things together.

On the other hand, Larry love, if you decide to be a total rat bastard and send this to Daddy, I'm going to drop the reins and give him his head. He has been telling me to have you thrown in jail for nonpayment of alimony. I have been telling him not to be silly, because how could you earn money to pay me if you were in jail? Still, prison would keep you from mailing any objectionable letters, so if you force my hand, you'll get locked up, darling.

You can still send *me* letters, though. Stories about your various escapades and all. I'd like to hear more about your role as Mad Poet with those damsels, for example. It's something to read whilst playing with myself. I've rediscovered masturbation lately, which should give you an idea of the social swim here in Richmond. Incidentally, masturbation is a lot more fun when you're old enough to know what you're doing. Like youth, it's largely wasted on the young.

I'll call you when I get to town.

Lisa

74 Bleecker St.
New York 10012
June 29

Miss Rozanne Gumbino
311½ West 20th Street
New York 10011

Darling Rozanne,

You'll note that I am not writing this letter on my official *Ronald Rabbit's Magazine for Boys and Girls* stationery, nor am I sending it to you at your office. That's because it is not official company business. On the contrary, this is a personal letter from me to you, from a man to a woman, and thus I am using ordinary typing paper and sending it to you at your home.

The reason I am writing you, Rozanne, is to provide you with transcripts of several telephone conversations I've had over the past few days. Perhaps you have already made notes of these conversations. If so, then this letter is a waste of time for both of us. But you seemed so agitated when I talked to you that it occurred to me that you might have failed to make a permanent record of the conversations, and so it seems worth the risk of duplication to put this down in writing for you.

I'm sure you'll appreciate that I am rendering the conversations in simple dialogue, without identifying the two speakers. This is precautionary, to prevent identification of the speakers should the letter fall into alien hands.

"Hello?"
"How do I know that's all you'll do?"
"Who is this?"
"What I mean is, if I knew that was all you wanted to do, if I thought I could trust you—"
"Oh, hello there!"
"You know who this is?"

"Yes, I think I do. I think I've heard this voice over the telephone before."

"Yes, telling you to come to his office."

"Yes, indeed. It's as though the earpiece of the telephone suddenly filled up with tits."

"You shouldn't talk like that!"

"Tits, tits, tits."

"Oh, my God."

"Tits, tits, tits. Did you get my letter? The offer still holds."

"You're really terrible, aren't you?"

"Not to those who know me."

"The thing is—"

"Yes?"

"Oh, my God."

"I think you've got the wrong number. This is the Mad Poet of Bleecker Street."

"I know who it is."

"For a minute I thought—"

"Listen to me."

"I'm listening."

"What you wrote in your letter. Are you listening to me?"

"I'm all tongue."

"What did you say?"

"Ears. I'm all ears."

"That's not what you said."

"True."

"I ought to hang up."

"I was thinking the same thing."

"If I thought you meant it—"

"Of course I meant it."

"I mean if I thought that was as far as it would go, if it would be just that—"

"Yes?"

"I have to hang up."

"Tits, tits, tits."

"I'm hanging up. I can't listen to any more of this. I'm hanging up."

"Tits and cunt, tits and cunt—"

"Good-bye."

"Hello? Hello, is anybody there?"
"Hello."
"Don't tell me, let me guess. It's the girl with all the tits."
"You make it very hard for me."
"Au contraire, ma chérie. You make it very hard for me. I've got it right here in my hand."
"Oh, my God, the way you talk!"
"Aren't you ashamed that you love it?"
"Oh, stop it."
"All right."
". . . Hello?"
"I'm still here."
"Listen to me."
"I'm listening."
"Oh, my God, I know what I want to say but I can't even say it."
"Give it another try."
"If I thought—"
"If you thought you could trust me—"
"Yes."
"—to just eat your juicy little cunt—"
"Yes, yes."
"—and if you thought I would stop there and not try to screw you—"
"Yes, yes—"
"Then what?"
"Huh?"
"If you could trust me, really trust me, then what?"
"You know."
"Then you might be interested."
"Maybe."
"How old are you?"
"What does that have to do with it?"
"Probably nothing. Don't you remember?"
"I'm twenty-six."

"Uh-huh. I guess you lived at home for a long time and now you have your own place."

"How did you know?"

"The Phantom knows everything. He has spies everywhere. Are you a virgin?"

"What does that have to do with it?"

"Probably nothing, but I guess you don't remember that, either, huh?"

"Suppose I am."

"I already supposed you were. When you play with yourself, do you like to pretend your finger is a tongue?"

"I'm hanging up now."

"I bet you're playing with yourself right now."

"I'm hanging up."

"You can trust me, you delicious cunt."

"Trust you? I can't even talk to you."

"Oh, I don't know. You've been doing pretty well."

"I have to go now."

"Come on over and I'll eat you."

"But you would want to do other things."

"That's not what you're afraid of."

"What do you mean?"

"You're afraid you would want to do other things."

"No, no, no—"

"I'll tell you what. I won't rape you even if you beg me to. How's that?"

"Oh, Mary and Joseph."

"Don't forget St. Anthony. Do you want me to put the promise in writing?"

"You're an awful person."

"I'm fun in bed."

"Stop it."

"I'm more fun than a finger."

"Oh—"

"I really am."

"I have to go now."

"I know, you have to wash your hands."

"Good-bye."

"Hello?"

"Hello."

"I was wondering when you'd call."

"Listen, I just wanted to tell you that I'm not going to call you any more."

"And you called to tell me that?"

"Oh, you always twist everything I say."

"Why don't you put the phone to your pussy? I think these conversations would work better if we didn't have to detour them through your brain."

"That's a terrible thing to say."

"You put the earpiece of your phone to your cunt, and I'll lick the mouthpiece of mine. How does that sound?"

"I'm hanging up."

"And you're never calling again."

"That's right."

"I'll look forward to hearing from you, my proud beauty."

Well, that's the way it went, Rozanne. I suppose you'll call again in a day or so, but in the meantime I wanted to type all of this up and send it to you so you would be able to avoid repeating yourself in future conversations. And now that I've got you on the phone, in a manner of speaking, I'd like to tell you a story of what happened this past weekend.

I had a house guest. An apartment guest, really, since I don't have a house. You might say that I don't have much of an apartment, either. You might say that what I had this weekend—just this Saturday, actually, she arrived Saturday afternoon and left Sunday morning—was a hovel guest. The hovel was so dismal that we spent almost all of our time in bed.

My hovel guest was a fifteen-year-old girl named Naughty Nasty Nancy Hall. You might be interested to contemplate the fact that she is eleven years younger than you are and stopped being a virgin over two years ago. I don't know what contemplating this fact will do for you, but it's something to think about.

You may have already read something about Naughty Nasty Nancy. It gets difficult to remember just what letters I sent to what places, and of course I may have left a copy of those letters around the Xerox machine, in which case they might have passed over your desk and beneath your gaze. At the risk of repeating myself, I'll refer to copies of past letters and include what observations I've already made about Naughty Nasty Nancy.

'We're sixteen. Except Naughty Nasty Nancy, who is fifteen.'

"'A mere child,' murmured Naughty Nasty Nancy. She was one of the two in the back seat, and wore a peaked witch's cap and granny glasses."

"In the back seat Naughty Nasty Nancy sat directly behind Dawn. Naughty Nasty Nancy does not speak too often, but her occasional remarks are always incisive. There is a distinctly fey quality to this girl, Steve. If you were casting Hamlet, you would pick her instantly for Ophelia."

"'I couldn't remember whether you wore jockey shorts or boxer shorts,' Alison said, blue eyes sparkling and plump cheeks glowing. 'But Naughty Nasty Nancy remembered.'

"'Hardly the sort of thing she'd forget,' B.J. said.

"'Meow,' said Nancy Hall. She was still wearing the witch's hat, and mordant madness danced in her eyes. 'Meow, meow, meow. Look at Merry Cat, she's positively radiant. Orgasm brings the most beatific look to her face. Are you in a state of grace, Mary Katherine?'"

". . . We all watched for a while, and Naughty Nasty Nancy kissed B.J. on the neck and touched her breasts, and Alison petted Naughty Nasty Nancy gently on the bottom. . . ."

There may have been a couple of other references to Naughty Nasty Nancy Hall, but those are the only ones I can spot readily, and they should refresh your memory if you've already read this material or put you in the picture if you haven't. What I want to tell you about, Rozanne, is what happened with Naughty Nasty Nancy at my place Saturday night and Sunday morning.

I won't bother describing the apartment. You'll see it for yourself when you finally get up the courage to come over and let me eat your box. Nor will I bother describing what went on for the first hour or two that Nancy (I'll call her that for short) spent in my bed. I'll just say that I licked her all over her body and then had prolonged intercourse with her. We shifted from one position to another on a sort of Cook's Tour of the *Kama Sutra*. Throughout all of this, Nancy remained active and supple and industrious, and glee glinted in her gray-green eyes.

But somewhere along the way, Rozanne, I began to get the feeling that something was missing. Nancy was enjoying herself, but I wondered if perhaps she wasn't enjoying herself a little less than she possibly might be. To construct a metaphor that you should appreciate, it was as if I had prepared a great plate of spaghetti for her but had stupidly failed to put any oregano in the sauce. It tasted *good* to her but it just didn't taste *right*.

And this perception made it impossible for me to continue. Not physically impossible—I remained quite the upstanding citizen, actually—but spiritually impossible. And so I withdrew from the choicest part of Naughty Nasty Nancy, who is indeed a collection of choice parts, who is in fact a synergistic young woman whose (w)hole is greater than the sum of her parts, and I propped myself on an elbow and my cock on her thigh and looked long and searchingly into her baby gray-greens.

"Is something the matter, Larry?"

"You stole my line."

"I don't follow you."

"You just did it again. Something's the matter, and you don't follow me. Am I doing something wrong?"

"Of course not."

"But I seem to have left out the oregano."

"I think I must have missed the opening credits," she said. "I don't get it."

"That's just it."

"I mean, I'm having a wonderful time."

"But there's something you like that I'm not doing."

"Not exactly."

"That means yes."

She put her hand on my cheek. Her hand was cold and dry. I brought her fingers to my lips.

"I don't always come, if that's what you mean. I can enjoy it without that."

"But you sometimes come."

"Sometimes."

"Just with girls?"

"No. In fact I usually have a better chance with boys. I'm not really into girls that much, to tell you the truth. None of us really are. It's having nothing but girls around all the time, and also that we love each other very much, and if you love someone you ought to love them physically. And also it feels good."

"Uh-huh."

"So it's not that."

"It's something special that you like to do."

"Sort of."

"So tell me and we'll do it.

"Well, you might not want to, Larry."

"Only one way to find out."

She turned her eyes away from me. "The thing is that it's perverted."

"Most everything is."

"Well, more perverted than most."

"So?"

She looked at me again. She was having trouble saying this, but her eyes still reflected a good measure of delight and amusement.

She said, "The thing is, it has to hurt."

"Ah. *Naughty Nasty Nancy.*"

"That's the idea."

"Whom does it have to hurt?"

"Me. Although—"

"Yes?"

"When I get off, I can go a little bit crazy. Biting and scratching and things like that."

"Sounds interesting."

"Also damned antisocial."

"So let's do it."

"It doesn't turn you off? Oh, my, I guess it doesn't. How big and hard it is. Do you really want to?"

"Yes."

"Okay." She took a breath, and I watched her face change. Her mouth slackened and her eyes glazed slightly. "Lie on your back, that's right. No, spread your legs. Now get inside me. Oh, God, you're so big and hard, and now I'll put my legs together and squeeze you. Can you feel how tight I am around you?"

(I could, Rozanne. I could.)

"Now hook your feet around my ankles. That's right, so I can't move. Now spank me."

"On the bottom?"

"Yes, right on my ass. Don't move your hips, don't move your cock around, just do everything with the spanking."

"How hard?"

"As hard as you can. And if I say to stop or if I yell that it hurts, don't pay any attention to me. Just go on hitting me harder. Use your other arm to hold me so I can't move. Yes, that's right. Now start beating the shit out of me. Oh, yes. Oh, Jesus. Naughty naughty naughty. Oh, naughty girl. God! Oh, you're killing me! Oh, Jesus Christ, stop, you're killing me, naughty, naughty, don't stop, harder, oh, Jesus, *oh*—"

She had an absolutely overwhelming orgasm.

She wasn't the only one, Rozanne.

Now you may be wondering why I took the trouble to tell you all this, Rozanne. You might even suspect that I simply wanted to write something that would get you all hot and bothered. I'll admit that the thought did cross my mind that you might well read this letter with one hand tucked up under your skirt. In fact it pleases me to picture you that way.

But there's more to it than that. You see, you want very much to come over and have me eat your pretty little cunt, but you're afraid I'll make a stab at your virginity. Or that I'll be upset with you for wanting only to be eaten. So I offer this story as proof that you can trust me.

Naughty Nasty Nancy wanted to be spanked. So I spanked her. Because it was what she wanted. And, simply because it was what *she* wanted, it became what *I* wanted, and I enjoyed the whole process as much as she did.

Think of me as an instrument for your pleasure, Rozanne. I don't know why you're afraid of losing your cherry. I don't have to know why, any more than I care why Nancy Hall can only come good when someone is reddening her rump. People who get hung up on why, wind up losing all their whats.

Call me. You can trust me. I'll give you more fun than you've got fingers.

Luckily,

Pierre

cc: Mrs. Lisa Clarke

Mr. Clarke You are behind your rent. Landlord says you owe two months says pay up rite away or out you go and the missus both.

Sup't

c/o Gumbino
311½ West 20th Street
New York 10011
July 4

Mr. George Ribbentraub
Ribbentraub Realty Corp.
414 East 14th St.
New York City

Dear Mr. Ribbentraub:

Let me take this opportunity to wish you and yours a happy Fourth of July. Of course the Fourth will have come and gone by the time you read this, but it is that very day now as I write this, and I can honestly claim to be moved by the spirit that inhabited the breasts of our founding fathers when they struck a blow for liberty and freedom.

While I might have wished you a Safe and Sane Fourth in any case, I must confess that the main purpose of this letter is to apprise you of the fact that I have permanently vacated premises at 74 Bleecker St. I am accordingly enclosing herewith two keys, one to the vestibule and the other to the apartment. Another set of keys remains in the possession of my wife, Mrs. Laurence Clarke. She may be reached c/o American Express, Cuernavaca, Mexico. I don't know the zip code, nor do I know whether appeals to her for the return of her set of keys are likely to meet with success. I tend to doubt it, as I have had no luck thus far in persuading her to send me $1480, which she seems to have taken along, like the keys, quite by mistake.

I trust you will cancel my lease forthwith and will retain my one month's security deposit in lieu of back rent and any other obligation that is mine under the terms of the lease. While it might dismay you to do this, I can really see no alternative for you, as I am presently unemployed, have no job prospects in the offing, and retain no cash assets.

As a sweetener, I have left all my furniture at 74 Bleecker St. Two appraisers have set a value of these goods, with one estimating their worth at $1480 and the other placing the figure at $520. Whichever figure one accepts, it seems fairly clear that you will be recovering furniture in excess of any monies owed you under the terms of the lease. I hereby deed this furniture to you in return for past and future favors.

Should this be unsatisfactory to you, you might attempt to reach a more pleasing settlement through contact with my attorney. He is Roland Davis Caulder with offices at 437 Piper Blvd. in Richmond, Va. While I have heard that disbarment proceedings against Mr. Caulder are in the offing, I am sure he will be able to represent me in his present capacity at least for the next several months.

I should advise you, however, that should you contemplate formal legal action against me, I would have no choice but to inform the appropriate authorities of the innumerable violations now in existence at 74 Bleecker St., and would further feel it incumbent upon me to notify Mrs. Ribbentraub of your liaisons with several tenants of those premises, among them my wife.

I trust you will take this advice in the spirit in which it is offered.

Best personal regards,
Laurence Clarke

P.S.: It might profit you to plan on engaging a new superintendent for 74 Bleecker St. The present holder of that post is under consideration for an important editorial position at Whitestone Publications, Inc., and you can hardly expect him to let his unswerving personal loyalty to you stand in the way of such an excellent opportunity for advancement.

L.C.

Larry or Pancho or whoever you are today,

You'll have to forgive me for being a little drunk as I write this. But if I weren't a little drunk, maybe more than a little, I couldn't write to you at all.

You bastard, you rotten bastard.

All you want to do is ruin things for Steve and me. That's fairly obvious. Just because we are two good people with a chance for happiness you have to be a little fox and spoil the vineyard. It makes me wonder why I ever thought I loved you in the first place. How could anybody possibly love a man like you? That is what I ask myself. Over and over I ask myself how could anyone ever love a man like you because you are no man at all, Larry, no man at all, you have no soul, and if someone cut you open there would be no heart in your body and that is how I feel about you, I swear it is.

Since your only goal in life is to make people miserable I am going to tell you that you are succeeding. Not that Steve and I are miserable because we love each other too deeply ever to be miserable, but we are getting there, thanks to you.

You are like a snake with an apple except you are not good enough to be a snake, you are more like a worm, a worm in an apple and even the apple is rotten and so are you, Larry, you rotten bastard.

Because of you we find ourselves asking ourselves silent questions when we already know the answers, but you make it impossible for us to relax and enjoy our happiness because you plant little doubts in our minds and the doubts feed and fester like lilies that smell worse than weeds.

I wish I were not drunk so that I could tell you just how much I hate you. And no matter what you do that you will not succeed.

I want you to know that, Larry.

If you have the slightest speck of human decency left within you, you will stop writing to us.

Your wife,

Fran

c/o Gumbino
311½ West 20th St.
New York 10011
July 9

Mrs. Laurence Clarke
c/o American Express
Cuernavaca, Mexico

Fran(ces)ca mi amore:

You ignorant cunt, if my letters bother you so much why did you just now open this envelope?

Or is it possible that they bother you in a necessary way? Think about that.

El Gringo

c/o Gumbino
311½ West 20th St.
New York 10011
July 9

Mr. Stephen Joel Adel
c/o American Express
Cuernavaca, Mexico

Dear Steve:

As you'll note, I am no longer living at 74 Bleecker St. I've given up the apartment and have signed over the furniture to my erstwhile landlord, a George Ribbentraub. I mention this because it's possible he may get in touch with Fran in order to recover her set of keys. If she has them on hand, you might suggest that she send them to him at Ribbentraub Realty Corp., 414 East 14th St. I don't know the zip code.

But that's nothing to be overly concerned about, Steve. In a way my change of address is linked to the subject of this letter, but that will become more apparent as you read on, and as I write on.

The thing that bothers me, Steve, and that has caused me to resume writing to you after having more or less determined to discontinue our correspondence, is that I have been given to understand that things are deteriorating between you and Fran.

And this bothers me.

To be frank, it bothers the hell out of me. Much as it hurt me to be deprived of my wife and my best friend in one swell foop, I was able to stand it because I was comforted by the thought that you were both involved in a total love relationship that transcended anything you could have had independent of one another.

Now it seems that you aren't getting along so well.

Well, this sort of thing happens all the time, Steve. It seems to have begun rather quickly with you two, but maybe that's all to the good. The sooner trouble rears its ugly head, the sooner you can reach out with your terrible swift sword and lop that ugly head clean off.

Listen, old buddy, don't bother to tell me that everything's roses with you and Fran. I know better. As a matter of fact, I may know better than you do.

Fran sent me a letter. Undated. (I wish you people would get in the habit of dating your letters. It only takes a second and simplified things all around.)

A depressing letter, Steve. I'm enclosing a Xerox copy of it so that you can read it for yourself and see how bad things really are. I wish I had Fran's letter here so that I could refer to it, but Rozanne took it along to the office with some other documents so that she could Xerox them. I used to do my own Xeroxing, but Rozanne pointed out that I was taking unnecessary risks by so doing. This is simpler, and saves me the trip to and from West 44th Street.

She'll be back around five-thirty, and by then I should be done with this letter, and I'll enclose the copy of Fran's letter and get the works into the mail.

Read Fran's letter, my oldest, dearest friend.

Read it and weep.

Done weeping? Good. Dry your tears, Steve, and sit back so I can do you a favor.

And I'm not kidding about this, either.

You know, both you and Fran have gone to great lengths to impugn my motives. It sort of tears me up to realize that both of you, two people to whom I have been very damned close, are so willing to believe I'm some kind of an ogre. I can't understand it. Rozanne loves me, Jennifer loves me, the daughters of Lancaster think I'm the greatest thing since the Pill, but my wife and best friend can't stand the written word of me.

Well, I think it'll be pretty obvious that I have no ulterior motive in writing this letter. My motive, and there's nothing the least bit ulterior about it, is to give you some information that will make it easy for you to restore things between you and Fran to the way they once were. More than that, I think you can actually raise your relationship with Fran to new heights.

What do I get out of this? Well, the satisfaction of having helped you both out. And the comforting knowledge that I haven't lost my wife and best friend for nothing.

I don't know if you know anything about Rozanne. Among the things she took to the Xerox machine this morning were a few letters to and from her, including one which I sent a carbon copy of to Lisa. (You remember Lisa.) There's no description of Rozanne in any of those letters, largely because I didn't know what she looked like, except for her mammary endowment, which is the first thing anyone would think of noticing about her.

I know you've always been partial to large breasts, Steve. That was one thing that surprised me about your running off with Fran, incidentally. Oh, she's not flat-chested, not by any means, but a man wouldn't take a look at Fran and automatically ask for a glass of milk. I always thought of her breasts as small but honest. For my own part, I've never cared that much either way. I like large breasts on large-breasted girls and small breasts on small-breasted girls. What I like, when all is said and done, is girls.

But one look at Rozanne and a guy like you would begin to salivate. The easiest way to describe it for you, Steve, is like so— picture your ultimate unattainable ideal in tits, improve on it, and you've got Rozanne.

(The hell you do. *I've* got Rozanne. You've got Fran, buddy.)

Aside from her breasts, Rozanne is just an average beautiful girl. Long black hair, dark complexion, fierce eyebrows, deep, liquid dark-brown eyes, and a strong nose and chin. A slim, supple body that is far too slim and supple for those breasts (but who's complaining, right?) tapering to a tiny waist and widening to a perfectly round ass. Hips designed for easy childbearing and joyful childconceiving. Good legs. Not great legs, but damned good legs. A nice little Italian girl from the Bronx. A nice little Italian virgin living all by her lonesome in Chelsea and working as secretary to a eunuch who, for some unaccountable reason, never had the gumption to flip her onto her desk and fuck her eyes out.

That's Rozanne. Now, to further set the stage, read the rest of the Xeroxed letters.

Okay. Now you're set for your lesson, even as Rozanne was set for hers. No more delaying tactics. We'll get right to the point.

After I wrote her the letter about Naughty Nasty Nancy, I figured one of two things would happen. Either I would hear from her almost immediately or I would never hear from her again. I figured either of the two developments would constitute a consummation devoutly to be wished.

A day or two after I mailed the letter, my phone rang. I picked it up, and the conversation went something like this:

"Hello?"
"Hello."
"*Aha!*"
"I got your letter."
"I hoped you would."
"How can you write letters like that? I mean, how can you do it?"
"It's a talent, I guess."
"It was here waiting for me when I came home from the office. I must've read it three times, maybe more."
"Did you masturbate?"
"Can't you talk nice to me?"
"I could, but you get more of a kick out of it when I talk nasty."
"How do you know so much about me?"
"Intuition, I suppose."
"I never met a man like you."
"Neither did I."
"Can I—"
"Yes?"
"I can't say it."
"You want help?"
"Yes."

"You want to come over here, don't you?"

"Yes, yes."

"Come right over."

"Shall I, uh—"

"Yes?"

"Well, couldn't you at least meet me somewhere, or something?"

"I'm not sure I would recognize you. Come up to my apartment, Rozanne. It'll save time."

"I guess so."

"I'll expect you in a half hour."

"All right, if I can get a cab."

"A half hour. Don't be late."

"Yes, yes."

She was early. I took a shower first, dried off, and fished around in the closet until I found a robe. It was practically new. I don't think I had ever worn it. Lisa gave it to me for my birthday once, or maybe it was Fran. (That gave it to *me*, I mean. Not that Lisa gave it to Fran. An ambiguous construction that I wanted to clear up.) I wonder if any man ever bought a bathrobe for himself. Or if any man ever wore the bathrobe his wife bought him.

I put the robe on with nothing under it and waited for her to turn up. She turned up, knocking timidly at the door. I opened it, and there she was.

"Hello," she said.

"Why, hello." I said. She was wearing a knit dress. It was red, and so tight that it looked like a blush. "You look good enough to eat," I said, and her face turned the same shade as the dress. "Come in," I said, and she came in, and I closed the door and locked it. She winced as I turned the lock, as if it meant she couldn't change her mind now. Which was precisely what I had been thinking.

"Now what?" she said. "Do I just lift up my skirt and you'll do it or what?"

"Is that what you think you want?"

"Well, I don't know. I'm new at this."

"You silly," I said, and kissed her.

She really didn't want to respond to the kiss, Steve. She wanted to get eaten and have an orgasm, but she was so tense she couldn't have had a Coke, let alone an orgasm. So I took a lot of time kissing her, and then I put some music on the radio, good old WPAT, nice mood music that you could fuck to without listening to.

(What do you do for music to fuck by in Cuernavaca?)

And we gradually worked our way to the bed, and I gradually got her out of her dress and paid the proper sort of homage to various parts of her anatomy. She kept saying that she knew she could really trust me, and I kept earning that trust by taking my time with her, being very gentle, very gentle, ever so gentle.

The poor kid had never really relaxed with sex before. She always dated these louts who would kiss her hard enough to bruise her lips, then grab her tits to test their grip, then make a beeline for her twat. She never had a chance to enjoy necking because she was too hung up with fears of what it would lead to.

Now she had her chance, and she was making the most of it. As I ran my tongue along the undersides of those incredible breasts and listened to her purr and throb, as I stroked the satin skin on the insides of her taut thighs, I thought how incredible it was that this girl had managed to maintain her hymen to the ripe old age of twenty-six.

"You can trust me," I said from time to time.

"I know I can trust you," she said now and again.

"I swear on my mother's life that I shall not penetrate your quim today, even if you decide you want me to."

"You're a gentleman, Larry."

"Of course you can change your mind at some future date, but not today. You walked into this apartment a virgin. You'll walk out of here a virgin."

"A gentleman. Oh, do that some more, it's wonderful. A real gentleman. I never met anyone like you before, never in my whole life. Oh, God, do you know what it does to me when you do that?"

I had a fair idea.

One thing, Steve. I *meant* that oath, and the fact that my mother died several years ago doesn't detract from it a bit. I used that wording for the impression it would make, not out of some perverse streak. (You and Fran seem all too willing to believe I have a perverse streak.)

Anyway, the oath couldn't have been any more binding had I had a living mother. I was determined not to violate that maidenhead. Rozanne was providing me with a rare enough pleasure anyway, the pleasure of slow seduction.

I didn't realize until then just how much I'd grown to miss that pleasure. That's one of the unfortunate by-products of the sexual revolution, Steve. There's no more working up to it. A girl either fucks or she doesn't, and the two of you decide it in front, and if she does, you both get into bed and you do it, and if she doesn't, you go away and that's it.

Even with the daughters of Lancaster, the most precious angels on earth, there was no gradual pursuit. They knew the game and enjoyed playing it, and they didn't have to be conned into anything. There were some things they had to be shown, owing to relative inexperience on their part, and it's always fun to play teacher, especially with such willing and adept pupils, but it's not the same thing.

Don't get me wrong. I approve of the change in morals. Seduction as a steady diet is a bore. Artificial as hell, and hard on the nervous system.

Once in a while, though, I miss it. Maybe it's ninety percent nostalgia. Still, once in a while I miss it.

So I took a long and lazy time with Rozanne. I inspected every bit of her body, turned her this way and that, kissed her here and there. A dozen times along the way she was within a couple of yards of the orgasmic goal line, and each time I would change the subject and throw her physically offside and penalize her half the distance to the goal. I kept building her up and letting her down, until she reached a point where her blood-pressure level was dangerously high.

Until finally I said, "Now I'm going to eat your cunt."

And she said, "Thank God."

I'll do the Victorian novelist number and draw the veil here, old buddy. The modesty bit. Let's just say that she got what she came for and came what she got for.

And liked it.

A little while later, after she had stopped talking about how divine she felt and how she had dreamed about this but had never, even in her dreams, imagined it would be quite this good, after she had finished bathing my ego in a salve of words, she said, "But what about you, Larry?"

"What about me?"

"I know men have needs."

"Don't worry about it."

"But aren't you—"

"Frustrated? Tied up in knots?"

"Uh-huh."

"Of course I am. Don't worry about it. Let's talk a little."

"Because there must be something I could do."

"Later, perhaps. If you want."

"Of course I want to help you."

"But first let's talk. Why is it that you're so afraid of getting popped?"

"Getting popped?"

"Of not being a virgin any more."

"Oh, getting popped."

"Right."

"I didn't know what you meant at first."

"I understand. Is it that you're afraid of getting pregnant?"

"No, it's not that."

"Because they have pills for that sort of thing."

"I know."

"And they're a hundred percent effective."

"Oh, I know. It's not that."

"Some kind of sin thing? That good girls have to stay virgins until they get married?"

"No. I don't believe that anymore."

"Thank God."

"I lost my faith. I suppose I'm an atheist."

"So am I, thank God."

"As a matter of fact, I guess I'd respect myself more if I wasn't a virgin. I mean, it's abnormal, being a virgin at my age."

"It's certainly unusual."

"Yeah."

"Then what is it, Rozanne?"

"Well, it's an irrational fear."

"Oh?"

"I went to a psychiatrist once. Actually I didn't go to him, I went out with him on a date. We saw *Plaza Suite*. Have you seen it?"

"No."

"I didn't even know he was a psychiatrist when I dated him. Just that he was a doctor. His sister was married to my sister-in-law's cousin."

"Aren't they married anymore?"

"I guess they're still married. What difference does it make?"

"No difference at all. I'm sorry I interrupted."

"It's okay."

"You were saying about the psychiatrist?"

"Oh. When I wouldn't, you know, what you said, that I wouldn't get popped. He told me I have an irrational fear. That's how he put it."

"Of what?"

"Pain."

"Pain?"

"Pain."

"It only hurts for a minute."

"I know that."

"Sometimes, for a lot of girls, it never hurts at all."

"I know that."

"Then—"

"That's what irrational about it. I know all that, but knowing doesn't help. I lie awake nights thinking about getting popped and I start to cry at the thought. I guess you must think I'm pretty hopeless, huh?"

"Not at all."

"I know people who have a thing about heights, they won't look out a high window, they won't even have an apartment or work in an office on a high floor. That's another irrational fear. If I had my choice, I'd rather have that. At least I could let myself get popped like a normal human being instead of living like some kind of a nun."

"You've got a problem."

"Don't I know it."

"Perhaps someday you'll be able to face it," I said gently. "But not tonight."

"No, I guess not. No, not tonight. But—"

"What?"

"I wish I could do something for you."

"You can."

She licked her lips anxiously. I suspect she was thinking that what I had in mind would involve her lips, and I further suspect she was trying to decide whether it was something she really wanted to do. While she played that tape through her mind I took off my bathrobe.

"Oh, my God," she said.

"What's the matter?"

"The size of it. Of your, uh—"

"Cock," I supplied. "It's average, actually."

"Honest to God?"

"Well, I never measured it and checked the *Guinness Book of Records* or anything, but I think it's about average. It's nothing exceptional."

"It's the size of a cannon."

"Oh, nonsense."

"It is. It would kill a woman."

"It never killed one yet."

"It would split a woman in half."

"Don't be ridiculous. You can touch it, you know. It won't bite."

"It's as hard as a rock, too. Holy Mother of God, imagine putting this in a fifteen-year-old girl. I didn't know they were this big."

"They?"

"Cocks."

She went on talking like that, handling the subject of the conversation with both hands as she talked. As you may know, Steve, you can tell a great deal about a woman by the way she handles a penis. Sometimes I think it's a better index to sensuousness than actually fucking her. Bill Adams used to keep an abstract cock on his desk as a paperweight. It was a cylindrical iron bar. Outside of that, there was nothing particularly cocklike about it. Girls who came over to his desk almost invariably picked up the thing and fooled around with it. He did or didn't date them on the basis of their reactions to it. A pretty good test, he always said. One day a girl picked the thing up and smacked in rhythmically against the edge of his desk as she talked. Paula, her name was, and she was the one he picked out to marry. Which tells you as much about Bill as her behavior told about Paula, come to think of it. . . .

But to return to Rozanne. She went on with her fondling, doing a very good job of it. Her hands were soft, except for the tips of her fingers which were roughened from typing, which made a pleasant contrast. (Ellen Jamison plays the guitar, which makes for even more of a contrast.)

As she said, "What would you like me to do?"

"Well," I said, "there *is* something."

"Anything," she said, and her eyes modified the word.

"It's a little unusual," I admitted, "but there's no pain involved, certainly. I want you to get in a certain position, and then I want to just touch my cock lightly against your bottom."

"And then what?"

"Then I'll have an orgasm."

"Just from that?"

"It's all in the position you'll be in. It's particularly exciting to me, God knows why. Maybe I saw my parents in this position as a child or something. We could ask your friend the psychiatrist."

"I guess if I can have an irrational fear, you're entitled to an irrational thrill."

"That's a good way to look at it."

"Well," she said. "What's the position?"

I positioned her. On her knees on the bed, arms straight, palms of hands planted on the bed sheet, breasts hanging down like ripe fruit. I studied her from various angles, reaching out to touch and adjust, and provided a little heavy breathing.

"Perfect," I said, huskily.

Then I positioned myself behind her, kneeling. I reached around to cup her breasts momentarily. I would have needed the hands of a basketball player to do them justice. I played with the nipples until they stiffened, but that was all the excitement she showed.

"Divine," I murmured.

I stroked the cheeks of her bottom, pulled them gently apart, pressed them together again, pulled them apart, pressed them together.

"Magnificent," I cooed.

I spat silently into the palm of one hand and anointed my cock with saliva, then dried my hand on the sheet and went back to playing with her buttocks.

"Paradise," I moaned.

And then I stabbed my cock straight into her tight little asshole.

Christ, how she screamed! I'm still amazed nobody called the cops. *I* would have called the cops, and I *never* call the cops. But it was one hell of a shriek.

Once I was in, all the way in to the hilt, I clapped a hand over her mouth and pressed my body down upon her, flattening her on the bed. She was pinned like a butterfly. She couldn't move. She could struggle, and the more she struggled the better it felt, and for the longest time I just clung to her and let her struggle while I enjoyed it.

I almost dropped the ball right then and there. That old familiar tickle started building up in my balls, and all those little sperm cells wanted to rush out and win this one for the Gipper. I didn't go through any horseshit like figuring the multiplication tables in my head. I've never had much success with that sort of nonsense.

Instead, I met the problem head on. *You're going to fuck this helpless little girl into a blind stupor,* I told myself, *and you're going to be so busy ramming it home you won't have time to worry about coming.*

And that is precisely what happened.

As soon as she gave up the struggle, I started to throw it to her. I was about as gentle as Attilla the Hun. I gave her solid full-length strokes, delivering them as though it was my intention to knock her asshole through the top of her head. Once I had established a certain rhythm, I took my hand off her mouth. She wasn't going to scream anymore. She just lay there whimpering from the pain and begging me to stop and invoking various saints in the hope that they might intercede.

"Oh, merciful Heart of Jesus, he's killing me!"

Bang!

"Oh, Holy Mary, Mother of God, I'm on fire!"

Wham!

"Oh, Saint Anthony, blessed Saint Anthony, make him stop before I die!"

Pow!

Thank God she was an atheist.

Steve, old buddy, it took forever. There was a time, Steve, when I must confess I didn't think it was going to work. I knew it was perfect in theory but I didn't think it was really going to work in actual practice. And if it didn't work, of course, then I was making a horrible mistake and really fucking things up for Rozanne.

One thing I've learned, Steve, is that once you've crossed the Rubicon, you might as well march right on to Rome. Even if you strongly suspect you made a mistake. Better to follow through with a wrong decision than to try changing your mind after the ball is in the air. I may have mangled the metaphors there, but you know what I mean. You just don't switch horses in the middle of a Rubicon.

So I kept on flailing away at her, never slowing the pace, never breaking the rhythm, never easing up on the sheer brute force of it. Do that for a while and your back starts to ache. Do it a little longer and you worry that your pelvic bone isn't going to be able to stand it.

Do it long enough and a miracle happens.

I did it long enough, and the miracle happened. I had expected the miracle, I was counting on it, and that didn't make it any the less miraculous.

Because gradually she stopped not liking it, and gradually she began liking it, and then all at once we were over the top and into the homestretch, and she was shouting things like *"Fuck me!"* and *"Kill me!"* and *"Tear me apart!"* and wriggling her ass, not to escape but to cooperate, and just as she got there I put a finger on her clit and threw her off the cliff.

Christ, did she come! Her entire rectum quivered and undulated around my cock like a vibrating condom. I hammered three more strokes into her as she came, and at the end of the third the dam burst. My sperm was backed up clear to the Holland Tunnel, but she quivered and twitched and milked every drop of it out of me. You know how, when you come really great, your balls actually ache with it? (But of course you know. I'm not talking to a schoolboy, am I?)

A little while later, almost as an afterthought, I withdrew from her. There was this delightful plopping noise reminiscent of opening a champagne bottle. I stretched out next to her. She lay inert, her face on the pillow, her eyes closed, her forehead bathed in sweat.

Ultimately she opened her eyes and looked at me. Just looked at me.

Then, abruptly, she began laughing.

Not a giggle or a chuckle. A full-throated, wide-open, all-woman laugh. She roared.

"Talk about irrational fears," she said finally.

"Yeah."

"Jesus, I honestly thought I was going to die. And then I didn't die. And then I lived. I'm twenty-six years old. God in Heaven, I wasted twenty-six years."

"You really couldn't have done much for the first thirteen, anyway."

"Maybe not. What is it they say? *'If they're big enough, they're old enough.'* Is that what they say?"

"I've heard the phrase."

"If I have a daughter, that's what I'll tell her. But I'll never get a daughter from what we did, will I? It's considered perverted, isn't it?"

"I suppose so. Almost everything is."

"What do you call it? What we just did."

"Anal intercourse, I guess. Sodomy. Buggery."

"Isn't there a good word for it?"

"You mean a polite word? Those are all about as polite as you can get."

"I don't mean a polite word, I mean a *good* word."

"I don't know. Ass-fucking, I guess."

"Ass-fucking," she said, reflectively. "You fucked me in the ass."

"I certainly did."

"I liked it."

"You certainly did."

"You fucked me in the ass and I loved it. It was even better than when you ate my cunt. I think I have to go to the bathroom. I feel as though I just had an enema."

"You just did."

"That's what it feels like. I'll be right back. Don't go away."

She was back before the toilet stopped flushing. "Oh, my," she said. "I don't feel like the same person anymore. I feel very different. First you ate my cunt and then you fucked me in the ass and now I went and took a huge crap. And now look how I'm talking. I never talked like this before. I never said words like that aloud."

"But you said them inside your head when you played with yourself."

"How did you know that?"

"Everybody does."

"They do? I thought I was the only one. I used to worry about it."

"You can stop worrying."

"I already have. Are you going to fuck me in the cunt now?"

"Not tonight."

"Because of your promise? I'll release you from it."

"Because I haven't got the strength."

"Oh."

"And the first time ought to be a good one."

"I guess you're right. Will it hurt as much as this did?"

"Not a tenth as much as this did."

"Oh. You liked this, didn't you? What we did? Ass-fucking?"

"Couldn't you tell?"

"Uh-huh. You roared like a bull, do you know that? Larry? Have you done this a lot? With other girls?"

"Hardly at all."

"Honestly?"

"Honestly."

"Why?"

"They mostly don't want to."

"Are you serious? I guess you are. Why?"

"Afraid it will hurt. And they occasionally think it's disgusting."

"Do you think it's disgusting?"

"Not at all."

"Neither do I. I think it's the closest thing to dying and going to heaven. Can we do this a lot? I don't mean tonight, I know you're tired. I mean, when we see each other from time to time. Unless you don't want us to see each other from time to time."

"I want us to see each other often."

"That's good, because so do I. And I want you to fuck me in the ass whenever you feel like it, and I want you to feel like it a lot. I think I have to take a crap again."

"Be my guest."

Flush!

"If the word gets around," she said on her return, "the laxative market is going to collapse. A whole industry down the drain. Did you hear what I said? '*Down the drain.*' I can only make jokes by accident. When I try to say something funny it never works. Are you ready to go to sleep?"

"Well, I was more or less thinking along those lines."

"Could I sleep here? With you? Because I don't want to go anywhere."

"Sure."

"What it is, I don't want to be too far from a toilet. Also I want to stay with you. You don't mind?"

"Not at all."

"Good. Larry?"

"Hmmmmm?"

"I think I love you."

She certainly seems to. And it's the most delightfully un-
complicated sort of love, Steve. I moved into her apartment, and
she cooks me these marvelous meals of sweet-and-sour shrimp
and chicken fried rice and moo goo gai pan. She's a fantastic
Chinese cook. (Hates Italian food, throws up at the sight of a
tomato, can't stand grass because it smells like oregano.) Every
morning she toddles off to the office, and every afternoon she
toddles home, and we fuck a whole hell of a lot.

She doesn't care if I get a job. She doesn't care if I screw
other girls. She doesn't even care if I have them over to her apartment and screw them in her bed. Likes me to do it, likes me to
tell her all about it, what we said and what we did and what it
was like. Sometimes she sits cross-legged on the bed while I tell
her, sits there and plays with herself. It's a lot of fun to watch a
pretty girl play with herself. . . .

All she wants in the whole world is for me to fuck her. In the
mouth, between the tits, in the twat, under the arm, between the
toes, anywhere, anytime, anyhow. And up the old wazoo. *Especially* that last. Loves to take it there. It still hurts. Not as much
as the first time, but it still hurts.

I don't know what we'll do if it ever stops hurting. I suppose
we'll think of something.

Well, I talked it all over with Rozanne, and she agreed that I
had to share this discovery with you. It's not enough to love a
woman, to cherish her, to adore her. It's just simply not enough.

What you've got to do, Steve, is haul off and fuck Fran in the
ass.

Really sock it to her.

But for God's sake, *don't let her know about it in advance.* In
fact, be damned careful she doesn't get hold of this letter.

Because if you tell her what you want to do, or if you try to
build up to it gradually, it just ain't gonna come off properly.
No way, baby. Because the world is full of women who are totally stone-certain that the one thing they don't want is to be

buggered. Even the experimentally inclined ones tend to change their mind after it's in an inch or so.

Because it hurts.

Which, of course, is the whole point. First you burn their guts out, and then, just when they're sure they can't take any more of the pain, you surprise them with a wave of pleasure that really knocks them out because they weren't expecting it. And once you've done that, you own them.

I've been trying to imagine what my life might have been like if someone had whispered this secret to me in my formative years. (Come to think of it, Norman Mailer more or less spelled out this idea in a couple of things. Maybe the trouble is that the important lessons of life are the ones we have to learn on our own.)

But if I had known then what I know now, Lisa would never have wanted to part company. She would have been transformed from an aggressive, castrating ball-breaker into a thing of beauty and a joy forever. And Fran, if truly buggered (we did it once, and she didn't like it, so I hurried up and came quick and agreed never to try it again), would not be in Cuernavaca at this very moment.

Well, have the sense to learn from my experience. Wait for a night when you're sure you won't come prematurely. Warm her up plenty, get her in the mood. Tell her you want to try it doggie style.

And then, when she's waiting with open box, give her the surprise of her life.

Pow!
Wham!!
Bang!!!
She'll love you forever, old pal.

With the utmost sincerity,

Your Friend, Larry

cc: Nancy Hall

Miss Nancy Hall
Camp Arondequois
R.D. #2
Seaford, Vt.

Dear Nancy:

By now I trust you and Dawn are settled in and adjusted to your role as junior counselors. If you haven't formed any alliances yet with the boy counselors, let me give you both a word of advice. Watch out for the dynamite studs—i.e., the swimming counselor, the athletic director, and all the standard Greek-god types. They may look great, but they won't fuck well. It comes too easy to them and all they want to do is get in and come in a hurry and cut another notch on their cock and find some other girls. As they get older they may have possibilities, but not now.

Instead, pick out some agreeable freak and pitch him right over the center of the plate. The kind of guy you like immediately as a person but don't even think of in sexual terms. Because, unless you misplace your intuition and pick a stone-faggot, *he'll* be thinking of *you* in sexual terms, and that's what it's all about. Pick the kid running the nature hut, or the one who teaches arts and crafts. If he turns out to be a virgin, so much the better. He'll never forget you, and you'll be into a whole new scene.

End of lecture.

I'm enclosing a copy of a letter to Steve. You know about Steve. I think you'll get a kick out of this one. So will Dawn, but you especially, Nancy.

Have a good summer, kids. I envy you all that fresh air and sunshine. But New York does have its compensations, as you'll read.

Do you get days off there? If you can ever make it to New York, please do. You can always stay overnight at our place. Rozanne is anxious to meet you.

Madly and poetically,

Larry

c/o Gumbino
311½ West 20th St.
New York 10011
July 11

Miss Ellen Jamison
c/o General Delivery
Bryn Mawr, Pa.

Dear Ellen:

By now I trust you're settled in with your mother and her new husband. I also trust you remember I said I would write you c/o General Delivery. I'm also marking the envelope *"Hold for Pickup"* to prevent some overzealous postmaster from taking matters into his own hands. I know you're positive your mother wouldn't open your mail. But why tempt fate? At the least, you would have to invent something when she asked you who the letter was from. I've always found that it pays to tell the truth whenever possible. Since it's rarely possible, the idea is to minimize situations in which lying becomes necessary.

How are you getting along with your mother and her new husband? (I hate to keep calling him that, it's so damned depersonalizing, but although you must have told me his name several times, I can't remember it. I keep thinking Ralph, but that can't be right, can it? I'll call him Ralph in this letter just to save time.)

There is one problem you are going to have to face, one question you are going to have to answer. It is simply this—whether or not to fuck Ralph.

No point pretending the question won't come up. You're both sexual and desirable, honey, and you've got enough of a mother hangup so that you can't help being attracted to her men for purely competitive reasons. (I seem to recall discussing this with you.) So you are going to want to fuck Ralph and Ralph is going to want to fuck you. You will both also want *not* to fuck each other. That's where the conflict is.

Be grateful you're not a virgin anymore. That would just make things more complicated.

I can't tell you how to answer the question. What I *can* tell you is this: If you decide to fuck him, you've got to do it in a messless fashion.

(1) Your mother must not find out. This means that you must avoid discovery. It also means that you must be sure Ralph will not, through some misguided impulse, tell her himself. He could do this out of guilt, or he could throw it in her face out of sheer shitfulness. If there's the slightest chance he might do this, stay the hell away from him.

(2) Neither of you can fall in love with the other. I think you're sharp enough not to fall in love with Ralph. It would be a natural mistake for you to make, but fortunately you're sufficiently self-analytical enough to be forewarned. And if you make it sufficiently obvious that the whole thing is inconsequential to you, male pride should keep Ralph from falling in love with you. Unless he's a hopeless loser, in which case you ought to stay away from him in the first place.

End of lecture.

Things have been generally good for me lately. As you can see from the return address, I've moved slightly uptown and am living with Rozanne Gumbino. I think you read some of my letters about her during your defloration. Well, not during. Before or after.

Have a good summer, kid. I envy you all that fresh air and sunshine. But New York does have its compensations, as you know.

Do you ever get a chance to get away? If you can ever make it to New York, please do. You can always stay overnight at our place. Rozanne is anxious to meet you.

Madly and poetically,

Larry

c/o Gumbino
311½ West 20th St.
New York 10011
July 12

Miss Mary Katherine O'Shea
and Miss Barbara Judith Castle
Bar-Bison Dude Ranch
Altamont, New Mexico

Dear Merry Cat and B.J.:

By now I trust you are both settled in for the summer, riding spirited bays and roans and mucking out the stables. When I think of you on the horses, I wish I were your saddles. When I think of the stables, I am reminded of that furnished room in Darien.

May I offer some unsolicited advice? It is, after all, one of the prerogatives of old age. If you're not in the mood, just skip the following paragraph.

Here goes. The thing is, the two of you are very much involved with one another. As I'm sure you have already come to realize. This never constituted any enormous hangup while you were at school, because the other four daughters of Lancaster were around, and there were various males, myself not (I fondly hope) the least among them.

Now you're out in God's country with nothing much around but squares on vacation and cowboys on horseback. You may dig some of the cowboys—anything's possible—in which case there's no problem. You may even dig some of the squares, as far as that goes, in which case again there's no problem.

But it's also possible that you won't, and that there won't be any other interesting females around either, and that you'll have only each other.

If so, there's nothing to worry about. That's the whole point, there's nothing to worry about. The only worry is worry, to paraphrase FDR. Because you might start brooding that you're lesbians and that that's bad and all the rest of it. If you wind up spending the entire summer just balling each other, that's perfectly fine. It's much better than balling someone else whom you don't like, just to convince yourself you're straight.

End of lecture.

Things have been generally good for me lately. As you can see from the return address, I've moved slightly uptown and am living with Rozanne Gumbino. I think you read some of my letters about her.

Have a good summer, kids. I envy you all that fresh air and sunshine. But New York does have its compensations, as you know.

I don't suppose you'll ever get a chance to get away? But if the summer is a bummer and you quit early, please make it to New York if possible. You can always stay overnight at our place. Rozanne is anxious to meet you.

Madly and poetically,

Larry

c/o Gumbino
311½ West 20th St.
New York 10011
July 13

Miss Alison Keller
c/o General Delivery
Hicksville, Long Island, N.Y.

Dear Alison:

By now I trust you are settle in for the summer with your folks. I hope the painting is going well, and that the rest of the situation is not as bad as you thought it might be.

I also trust you remember I said I would write you c/o General Delivery. I'm also marking the envelope *"Hold for Pickup"* to prevent some overzealous postmaster from taking matters into his own hands. I know you're positive your parents wouldn't open your mail. But why tempt fate? At the least, you would have to invent something when they asked you who the letter was from. I've always found that it pays to tell the truth whenever possible. Since it's rarely possible, the idea is to minimize situations in which lying becomes necessary.

May I offer some unsolicited advice? It is, after all, one of the prerogatives of old age. If you're not in the mood, just skip the following paragraph.

Here goes. The thing is, it looks as though you're pretty sure to have a shitty summer. I wish you just the opposite, but in view of your intrafamily conflicts and your particular social role in Hicksville (and in view of Hicksville itself, which certainly must live up to its name) you and I both know that an idyllic summer is less than likely.

You may be tempted to try to work out some of these conflicts, to try to open things up and assert yourself a little. This sounds like an invitation to cop out, but I think you should, well, cop out. There's no way you can really resolve anything, and if you try you'll just make yourself (and everybody else) still more miserable. A vital part of the whole maturation process is learning when to cop out, and this is one of those times.

Take the frustration and put it into your painting. It's very important to develop a creative means of getting accumulations of garbage out of your head. I do it with a typewriter. You learned a long time ago to do it in paint, and you have the advantage of producing something beautiful, while all I do is write silly letters. Stay with it, Alison. Paint like a madwoman. I think you're phenomenally talented, for whatever it's worth.

Things have been generally good for me lately. As you can see from the return address, I'm still living with Rozanne. She knows you were here that day, by the way, and is perfectly agreeable about that sort of thing.

Have a good summer, kid. I envy you all that fresh air and sunshine. But New York does have its compensations, as you well know.

At least you'll be able to get away from time to time. Whenever you get a chance to come into the city, please do. You can always stay overnight at our place. Rozanne is anxious to meet you.

Madly and poetically,
Larry

WHITESTONE PUBLICATIONS, INC.
67 West 44th Street
New York 10036

From the desk of Clayton Finch, President

July 15

Mr. George Ribbentraub
Ribbentraub Realty Corp.
414 East 14th Street
New York 10003

Dear Mr. Ribbentraub:

Mr. Hector Carbo has given your name as a reference, and I would greatly appreciate your giving me any pertinent information on the man's employment record with you, plus any general remarks you might care to offer concerning his character and personal habits.

The post for which Mr. Carbo is under consideration carries a considerable load of executive responsibility and calls for keen all-around judgment and accomplished editorial skills. Should we decide to employ Mr. Carbo, he will take the helm of *Rachel Rabbit's Magazine for Girls and Boys*. This publication, while essentially a revamped version of a proven success, is in other respects a new venture entirely, oriented as it is towards Women's Liberation for the junior set. We feel very strongly about its potential, not only as a highly marketable item but as one which may beneficially influence contemporary American culture.

In this light, I would appreciate any information which may reflect on Mr. Carbo's suitability or lack thereof.

Warmest regards,

Clayton Finch

CF/rg

From the desk of Clayton Finch, President

July 19

Mr. Laurence Clarke
74 Bleecker Street
New York 10012

Dear Mr. Clarke:

You go too far, Mr. Clarke.

I had begun to think that this unilateral war directed against me was over. It seems you are determined to persist in it. As the result of your latest folly, I found myself entangled in a completely hysterical conversation with a person named Ribbentraub, who wanted to know why I wanted to hire some Puerto Rican janitor as a magazine editor. I had a great deal of trouble disengaging myself from this lunatic but ultimately managed to convince him of what I suspected myself, that the whole affair was the result of an innocent misunderstanding.

Innocent!

Mr. Ribbentraub, however, was not so easily put off. He promptly mailed me a letter which he had received, typed on my own letterhead with my own signature rather inexpertly forged on the bottom of it. I might still have been in the dark but for your use of the *Rachel Rabbit's* nonsense, which instantly identified the perpetrator of the deed as yourself.

I could even forgive this last, Clarke, but for an even more grievous effort on your part, which I uncovered only through further communication with poor Ribbentraub. I called him to attribute this madness to you, and to persuade him to give me your forwarding address. This he did, and I thus discovered that you had the temerity to supply him with the address of my secretary, Miss Gumbino.

For heaven's sake, Clarke, what's the point of this sort of nonsense? Why besmirch the name of an innocent girl simply to gratify your sense of the ridiculous? It accomplishes absolutely nothing. No one is fooled by your little performances, no one at all. I'm happy to report that I passed this information on to Miss Gumbino, who as you may well imagine was roundly shocked by what you attempted to imply. Fortunately, however, she was able to tell me that there have been no repercussions from your little prank, and that you have ceased to press your unwelcome attentions upon her. Perhaps you do have some element of decency in you. Hardly an abundance thereof, but some.

Nevertheless, you have gone too far, as I said above. I am thus obliged to tell you that, in the seemingly unlikely event that you eventually bestir yourself to seek gainful employment, it will no longer be possible for this office to provide you with a favorable reference.

How on earth did you manage to filch my personal letterhead, Clarke? No, don't tell me. I don't want to know. I don't want to hear from you or of you ever again. While I cannot go so far as to say that I wish your death, I must allow that your obituary is one I would read with some pleasure.

I am sending this letter to your old address. I assume you did not play the same odd prank on the Post Office that you visited upon Mr. Ribbentraub, and that this will reach you in due course.

Clayton Finch

CF/rg

Ribbentraub Realty Corp.
414 East 14th Street
New York, New York

"A Realty Corporation With A Heart"

July 20th

Mr. Laurence Clarke
c/o Gumbino
311½ West 20th Street
New York 10011

Dear Clarke:

All right already, you little bastard. This is to notify you formally that Ribbentraub Realty Corp. hereby formally agrees to termination of the lease on premises occupied by you at 74 Bleecker St., New York City, and further agrees that no obligation, financial or otherwise, exists between the parties.

You got what you wanted, you little son of a bitch. I fired that moron Carbo but hired him back again. You ever show up around 74 Bleecker and Carbo is probably going to break your fucking head for you.

As far as I'm concerned you're a dirty little son of a bitch, but credit where credit is due and all of the rest of it. Which is that I have to admit that you're one sharp little cocksucker.

You ever want a job, I can probably find something for you to do, you little bastard.

George Ribbentraub

GR/rls

Mrs. Lisa Clarke
c/o Mr. Roland Davis Caulder, Esq.
Muggsworth, Caulder, Travis & Beale
437 Piper Blvd.
Richmond, Va.

Dear Lisa:

Forgive me for writing you in care of your attorneys. I somehow misplaced your address, but knew that it would be safe to write you in this fashion. Certainly a man like your father would not dream of opening your mail, not with his high ethical standards.

Of course if he did open it, he would be sure to seal it in such a way that you wouldn't suspect a thing. Makes you stop and wonder, doesn't it?

But my purpose in writing is not to provoke you, much as you may think so. Actually I've mellowed lately to a degree which might surprise you. If you'll think back to your last letter, you were dead certain while writing it that I would pass it on to your father. As a matter of fact, I haven't passed it on to anyone. Of course Rozanne has read it, along with various people who have turned up at the apartment, but there's no reason for that to bother you.

As a matter of fact, it's that very letter that prompts me to write this one. For a couple of weeks now I've been expecting you to write or call or turn up on my doorstep, and was rather looking forward to a reunion with you. I know Rozanne has expressed an interest in meeting you, and it is an interest I share all the way.

I really expected you to show up this past weekend. You might say I was counting on it, and so was Rozanne. But fortunately we did have company, as it happened. Ellen Jamison turned up Saturday afternoon and stayed with us until just after lunch Sunday, when she had to catch a bus back to Bryn Mawr. While her presence wouldn't have made you any less welcome—Ellen has heard a lot about you and would like to meet you sometime—it might have been just the slightest bit awkward having two guests, as our space here on West 20th Street is somewhat limited. There's only the one bed, and four would be an awfully tight squeeze.

Well, if nothing else, Lisa love, I can at least tell you what you missed out on. You already know a lot about Rozanne, because I remember I sent you a copy of a letter I wrote to Rozanne herself. Suffice it to say that the situation worked itself out surprisingly well, and that the cloistered Italian virgin was turned into a sexual dynamo by the simple expedient of —

No, come to think of it, I'm not going to tell you how I did it. Some other time, perhaps.

You'll want a description of Rozanne, and of Ellen.

I've already described Ellen for you, but how do I know if you keep all my letters as faithfully as I keep yours? Here we go, from a letter I wrote to Steve Adel:

"On my right, Ellen Jamison, red-haired and slim-hipped and flat-chested and freckled. If her father ever loses his several million dollars, she can always earn a living posing for Norman Rockwell. She even has braces on her teeth."

And now a description of Rozanne, from another letter to Steve:

"But one look at Rozanne and a guy like you would begin to salivate. The easiest way to describe it for you, Steve, is like so—picture your ultimate unattainable ideal in tits, improve on it, and you've got Rozanne. . . .Aside from her breasts, Rozanne is just an average beautiful girl. Long black hair, dark complexion, fierce eyebrows, deep, liquid dark-brown eyes, and a strong nose and chin. A slim, supple body that is far too slim and supple for those breasts (but who's complaining, right?) tapering to a tiny waist and widening to

a perfectly round ass. Hips designed for easy childbearing and joyful childconceiving. Good legs. Not great legs, but damned good legs."

So there the three of us were in our apartment.

It was awkward at first, I'll admit it. See, Rozanne had never made it with a girl before, and she was nervous about it, and the nervousness was contagious, as nervousness so often is. We had talked about it, Rozanne and I, but talking about it is not the same thing as doing it.

Rozanne was all for it, actually. She liked to talk about what she would do in a situation like this, or have me talk about what the daughters of Lancaster had done with each other. Talking about it served as an exciting prelude to sex for her. But now Ellen was right there in the room, and we all knew we were all going to ball, and none of us were coming right out and saying so, and it created a certain degree of tension.

Rozanne asked what kind of a summer Ellen was having.

"A dreary one," Ellen said. "Perfectly drab. There are no people around."

I said, "I gather nothing happened with Ralph."

"His name isn't Ralph."

"I didn't really think it was, but I couldn't remember it for some reason."

"It's Ronald."

Rozanne said, "How could you forget that? Ronald as in Rabbit."

"It guess that's why I forgot."

"I wish I could forget," Ellen said. "He's Ronald Rabbit, all right."

"Oh, then something did happen."

"Barely. He came while he was on the way to the bed. It won't be hard to follow your advice about not falling in love with him, Larry. And he won't fall in love with me. He won't even look at me. My poor mother."

(Oh, I forget to tell you, Lisa. Ralph—I mean Ronald—is Ellen's mother's current husband. But not for long, if Ellen is to be believed.)

Well, that at least got the conversation around to the topic of sex. Next, I told Ellen to come over and give me a kiss because I had forgotten how braces tasted. (She wears them on her teeth.) (Where else?)

We have a long absorbing kiss, and then I went over and kissed Rozanne, and then I said, "Well, that's two sides to a triangle. Now why don't you two kiss and make out?"

Rozanne's face took on a troubled look. She had already told me once or twice that she could see herself doing all sorts of more obviously sexual things to a girl, but couldn't quite picture herself kissing one.

Ellen didn't share this hangup. She went right over and put her arms around Rozanne and kissed her full on the mouth, and I looked at the two of them, and all at once my pants felt too tight.

Rozanne's face was all flushed when the kiss ended, but whether this was from excitement or embarrassment I couldn't say. Perhaps a mixture of the two. She sighed and sat down on the edge of the bed and Ellen sat next to her and put her head on her shoulder. (Put her head on Rozanne's shoulder, that is to say. It's a lot easier to describe situations involving only one person of each sex, let me tell you. As soon as there are two girls in the game, pronouns start getting screwed up.)

Rozanne looked down at her, then put an am around her. "God," she said, "you're just a kid."

"I know."

"It's scary."

"It must be," Ellen said. "After all, you're old enough to be my older sister."

"Well, when you put it that way—"

"Have your breasts always been that big?"

Rozanne's color deepened. "I wouldn't say *always*."

"When?"

"Well, just about since I was your age. Wait a minute, let me think. You're sixteen? No, they were still growing then, because I went to an E cup just two months after I turned seventeen."

"Somehow I'm not encouraged. An E cup!"

"Right now I'm not wearing anything. Larry doesn't like me to wear a bra. He says he likes to watch me bounce."

"I don't blame him."

"But I have to at the office. It's a rule they have; everybody has to wear a bra."

"Even the men?" I put in. But neither of them paid any attention.

"I don't blame *them*, either," Ellen said. "If you bounced around the office, nobody would get any work done. I'm not wearing a bra either. Big beastly deal. There's nothing to bounce. When I don't wear a bra, nobody notices."

"Well, don't let it get to you, Ellen."

"I wish I was built like you."

"Are you kidding? I used to walk around feeling like Elsie the Cow. And the men are terrible. I wouldn't mind if they just wanted me for my body, but it wasn't even my body, it was a small part of my body."

"Small?"

"I mean, it's no fun going through life following your tits from room to room."

"I suppose. I hope I'm not bringing you down now, making such a fuss over them, but I can't help it."

"No, of course not."

"They're beautiful. Pardon me, *you're* beautiful."

"So are you."

"Oh, please."

"You're adorable. You make me feel all funny inside."

"Honestly?"

"Cross my heart."

"May I cross your heart?" Ellen grinned impishly and drew a cross with the tip of her finger, first a vertical line from the hollow of Rozanne's throat down almost to her waist, then a horizontal line from one nipple down the slope of the breast and across the forbidden valley and up the slope of the other breast to its nipple.

"Oh," Rozanne said.

"Maybe you wouldn't mind taking your sweater off."

"First kiss me."

They kissed and Ellen's hands fastened on Rozanne's breasts.

"Oh," Rozanne said again.

"Now take your sweater off."

"Yes."

"In fact, maybe you could take everything off."

"That's a very good idea. You, too."

"Sure."

"I was afraid I wouldn't be able to relax with you. I was afraid I wouldn't be able to get in the mood."

"And?"

"Silly of me."

"Oh, Rozanne!"

"Just the way you look at my tits makes me hot. Do whatever you want to me. Anything."

"Lie down. Do you like when I touch them? I want to kiss them. Your nipples are bigger than my breasts. My mother didn't breast-feed me. God forbid that anything should happen to her precious figure. That, and my mother hangup, and not having a decent figure myself—"

"I like your figure. I like your body."

"But being flat-chested, I guess I have a breast fixation. It was never this obvious before, but then I never met anyone like you before. How can they be so firm and still be this big? I mean even when you lie down. I've never seen anything like it, it's fantastic."

"God, what you're doing to me."

"Do you mind if I just adore them for a while? I just want to kiss them and touch them. I want to curl up like a baby and suck your beautiful tits."

"Ohhhh!"

"Oh, wow, Rozanne. You like this, don't you?"

"God, yes."

"I'm going to be able to come just from this. I can feel it. Not touching myself or anything. Just lying here and sucking on you. I wish I had two mouths so that I could suck them both at once."

I had more or less decided to sit out this dance, Lisa, but that last remark was too much of an invitation. I walked around the bed and got on the other side of Rozanne from Ellen and popped

Rozanne's breast into my mouth. Well, popped the nipple in. Not even Martha Raye could have managed the entire breast.

What total contentment. Ellen and I were Romulus and Remus while Rozanne played Mama Wolf. Ellen, true to her word, reached a climax just from sucking Rozanne. Rozanne, who had made no predictions either way, had an orgasm just from being suckled.

I just had a good time. No climax, just a good time. Which was all right, because we had a whole night ahead of us, and I didn't want to use up all my ammunition in the first battle.

What a night, Lisa.

I could tell you who did what and with which and to whom, but I'm not sure I would remember everything or get it in the proper order, and besides I don't want to make this letter too long.

But you've always been an imaginative girl—I'll swear to that—and I don't doubt that you can exercise that imagination and get a good idea of what went on. Whatever you can imagine, we probably did it.

It's wonderful, how completely Rozanne overcame her inhibitions. Bisexuality came naturally to the daughters of Lancaster, as you may have gathered from past letters. Their school is at least partially responsible for this, and while I personally think that's easily the best thing to be said for the Convent of the Holy Name, I somehow doubt they would want it noised about.

The school wasn't the only factor, though. There's also a generational thing. I've gotten tired of hearing all this garbage about a New Morality, but that doesn't mean it doesn't exist. Kids are simply more open today than we ever were. Lisa, you and I were born too goddamned soon. Kids have so much more fun than we ever had during those years. They do things that feel good.

Rozanne, six years younger than me and ten years older than Ellen, is far closer to my generation than to Ellen's. Add to this her extremely cloistered upbringing and you generally have a girl who wouldn't say shit if she had a mouthful, as the feller says.

Well, she's certainly come a long way, even further than the girl in the Virginia Slims commercial.

At one point, pausing to glance up from between Ellen's parted thighs, she said, with an air of archimedic discovery, "You know, it would really be ridiculous not to enjoy doing this just because I happen to be a girl."

And then she went back to what she was doing.

Maybe it's just as well you didn't show up, Lisa. If you had been Rozanne's first experience, and if Rozanne had been your first experience as well, it might have been like two virgins on a wedding night. No blood on the sheets, but the same kind of awkwardness.

Or would it have been your first time?

Ah, well. Hardly matters now, does it? In any event, Rozanne's first time, like Rozanne herself, has come and gone. Gone shopping, as a matter of fact. She's down in Chinatown doing her marketing for the week. She always comes home with a couple of sackfuls of things that look as though she found them in a garbage can, and then she dices and slices and swirls them around in her wok, and the result is a meal fit for a mandarin.

A wok, for your information, is a shallow Chinese frying pan suitable for cooking things in a small amount of very hot oil. I mention this not to flaunt my culinary expertise but because it occurs to me, on reading the last paragraph, that you might not know the word and might think it a euphemism for cunt. Rozanne does lots of things with her cunt, but so far she hasn't filled it up with bean sprouts and water chestnuts.

Although, come to think of it, it just might beat soy sauce.

. . .

Inscrutably,

Julia Childs

Camp Arondequois
RD #2, Seaford, Vt.
July 19 or 20, I think. . .

Mr. Laurence Clarke
c/o Miss Rozanne Gumbino
311½ West 20th Street
New York 10011

Beloved and treasured Mad Poet—

Naughty Nasty N. and I absolutely flipped over your letter. *Quelle* brittle! Are Rozanne's breasts that much better than mine? I think I'm jealous!!

And NNN is jealous because you didn't do unto her as you did unto Rozanne. We're both afraid that our Mad Poet doesn't love us anymore, and if you're not terribly good to us we'll hire your first wife's father to sue Rozanne Gumball for alienation of affection.

Your advice got here too late—I'd already made the mistake of letting the lifeguard get to me. Beautiful romantic setting, full moon, blah blah blah. He gave me a totally boring fuck on the diving board and all I could feel was the burlap under my behind. It took forever for the marks to go away. He's a beautiful guy, great body, outstanding equipment, but no idea what to do with it. Wham, bam, and not even thank you, ma'am. He came before I even left, and then he let out this yell and flipped off into the pool!!! I'm not kidding, he really did!!! When I politely suggested that perhaps he could eat me, he announced that a real man never did a thing like that. Can you believe it????

All is well now, though. Miss Naughty Nastiness and I have connected with the camp's three stone-freaks, and if we don't all get fired it should be a dynamite summer. Three skinny guys with long hair and scraggly beards, but do they ever know where it's at!! They're also into each other, so the five of us get together for total group gropes now and then, which is fun.

Love ya,

Dawn

Hello, there, you Mad Poet you! This is Miss Hall speaking. I'm afraid we can't accept your invitation, as us slaves is not allowed to leave the ole plantation until the end of the season. Until the cotton is harvested, I mean.

You are our freaky Mad Poet and we love you. Kiss Rozanne for me.

Miss Hall

Me too! ! !

Dawn

Hi! Just wanted to get the last word in e
d
g
e
w
i
s
e
.
.
.

NNN

Mr. Laurence Clarke
c/o Gumbino
311½ West 20th Street
New York, New York

Dear Larry—

Greetings from the biggest horse's ass in Mexico.

You guessed it. Fran took off and left me, and I've spent the past few days in a drunken stupor. Tequila can really wipe a person out.

Now that she's gone and it's all over, I can see what a complete bastard I was. I went and fucked up the greatest friendship of my life for one month of kinging it in Mexico, and now where the hell am I?

Larry, I can't undo what I did, and what the hell is the point of saying I'm sorry? Especially when you already went ahead and forgave me. The best I can do is plead temporary insanity. That's what it was. I was literally out of my mind.

And so was Fran. I'm not putting any blame on her. We both managed to convince ourselves and each other that we were Romeo and Juliet all over again. Everything was at such a constant fever peak that of course it was all artificial and we couldn't stay at the peak all the time and when we fell it took forever to touch bottom because we started so high off the ground.

What I regret most of all is the things I wrote to you and the way I misinterpreted what you wrote to me.

What's really ironic is that the thing that finally killed our relationship was me trying to take your advice. I mean the advice in your last letter about doing it to her the way you did to Rozanne Gumbino. I mean, in the ass. Of course things had slipped to a pretty low state by then and maybe the end was inevitable, but taking your advice certainly brought things to a head.

The hell of it is that I honestly think your advice would have worked if I just could have brought it off properly. You just may have come up with the greatest discovery since the wheel.But I couldn't hang in there long enough. I gave her about a half a dozen strokes and shot my bolt, and at that stage all she was doing was screaming and trying to get away.

Well, that sure as hell tore it, fella. She lashed into me like I was the Markee de Sade, what a horrible man I was, how my true nature was now emerging, and all that crap. I didn't even try to explain. I thought, well, that's the end of it, and I guess deep down inside I was relieved. At least there would be no more of that off-again-on-again shit. At least it was over and done with and I could go out and get drunk, which is what I did. That tequila gives you a hangover that doesn't quit, and the only thing to do is go out and get drunk again.

I'm sober now, and I guess I'll stay that way because I can't afford much heavy drinking, even at Mexican prices. Wouldn't you know that she took every centavo with her, except for what I had in my wallet. Which is enough for me to live on, but for how long is anybody's guess. I can't afford to buy film, and if I don't have film I can't do any magazine assignments, so I may be stuck in this fucking hole for the rest of my life, and I guess I don't deserve much better than that.

Damn it all, it would have worked. What I'm going to do is wait here until I find a nice rich girl with big tits who's really looking for it, and then I'm going to fuck her in the ass until she can't see straight. No more six strokes and over. If it takes self-hypnosis, I'll try that.

Well, now you know how things are with your old pal. For what it's worth, thanks for trying to help. It's not your fault things went the way they did.

Adios, motherfucker,

Steve

Hicksville
July 22nd

Mr. Laurence Clarke
c/o Gumbino
311½ West 20th Street
New York 10011

Lovable Laurence,

CANNOT HACK HICKSVILLE. WISH VISIT YOU FRI-
DAY. ADVISE SOONEST IF POSSIBLE. WILL BRING DY-
NAMITE EROTIC PAINTING FOR YOUR APARTMENT.
IF THIS REALLY TELEGRAM INSTD LETTER IMPOS-
SIBLE TELL YOU LOVE YOUR GREAT BIG PENIS. LOVE
YOUR GREAT BIG PENIS.

Alison

c/o Gumbino
311½ West 20th St.
New York 10011
July 24

Miss Alison Keller
c/o General Delivery
Hicksville, Long Island, N.Y.

Dear Alison,

    COME AS SOON AS YOU CAN. ALL PUNS IN-
TENDED.

Sexual & Western Union

219 Maple Road
Richmond, Va.
July 23rd

Mr. Laurence Clarke
c/o Gumbino
311½ West 20th St.
New York 10011

Dear Ex,

You make a mistake, lover. Up to a certain point, your letters really were getting to me. So I thought I might drop in on you and see if we couldn't have fun in an old-friend-type way.

But you loused it up, because I guess you really don't understand little Lisa at all. You never understood me when we were married, so how you could understand me now is a good question.

Maybe orgies and switcheroos are what you and Miss Fettucine and your little schoolgirls enjoy. Maybe that's very much where it's at, and maybe my generation gap is showing. Frankly, my dear, I don't give a shit, as Rhett Butler *really* said.

Lisa is just an old-fashioned girl. I'm afraid. All I want is one man who knows he's a man and who's man enough to make me know it.

For a while there, even though I should have known better, I actually thought you might turn out to be that man after all. Maybe that's because you're a writer and tend to come across better on paper than you do in person. I don't know. But it was a mistake on my part, just as every man I meet turns out to be a mistake on my part, although I honestly sometimes think they're all really a mistake on God's part and not mine.

I know you think of me as a ballbreaker. You've made that perfectly clear often enough. Well, you're not the only man who ever came to that conclusion, and maybe I am a ballbreaker, but if so, it's only because every man I meet has unbelievably fragile balls. Hit a high note and they shatter to bits.

What I am, and all I am, is a woman. And what I want, and all I want, is a man who knows what to do with a woman when he finds one. A strong man, Larry. A man with real balls on him. A man that I can't break. A man that would break me instead, and put the pieces back together so that I could feel whole and complete for the first time in my life.

I don't know if Daddy read the letter before passing it on to me. A cute little game on your part but I'm afraid I'm not playing, because I really don't care. I'm sick of Richmond, it was a mistake to come here, but where the hell else would it be any better? I'd go to the moon if I thought it would do me any good.

I'm afraid you and Miss Arrivederci won't have the pleasure of eating fried rice out of my cunt, or whatever it is you're doing these days.

Ciao,

Lisa

c/o Patricia Kettleman
14 Fairfax
Albuquerque, New Mexico
July 23rd

Dear Larry,

Perhaps this is old news to you, but I have left Steve. I must have been insane to have anything to do with him in the first place. I guess I built him up in my mind as some kind of perfect person because I needed an excuse to get out of our marriage, which had turned bad for both of us. Talk about out of the frying pan and into the fire.

I won't go into details. I was already beginning to realize that he was not the person I thought he was, and then one night he did something absolutely inhuman. I can't even tell you what he did. I don't want to think about it, let alone put it on paper. Let me just say that it was horribly painful for me and that he went right on with it in spite of all my pleas.

I would ask you to take me back, but what is the point of it? We are no good for each other. In fact, the last thing I want is to look at a man. I always thought Women's Liberation was silly, but they really have got something. Men exploit women constantly, in and out of bed. It's a natural law of nature, though. All the picketing in the world isn't going to change it, but that doesn't mean a woman has to like it.

Sometimes I think I should have become a nun.

I'm staying with an aunt of mine. Patricia Kettleman. I don't think you ever met her. She was widowed three or four years ago. One of these days, if I get up the courage, I just might tell her how lucky she is.

Fran

MEMORANDUM

From: Laurence Clarke
To: Laurence Clarke
Date: 26 July
Subject: Various subjects

Aha!

L.C.

c/o Gumbino
311½ West 20th St.
New York 10011
July 26

Mrs. Lisa Clarke
219 Maple Rd.
Richmond, Va.

Dear Lisa:

I apologize.
For what?
For everything.
Lisa, your letter was an eye-opener. I wish you had said what you did years ago. Things might not have worked out any differently between us—you're absolutely correct in your estimate of the unbridgeable gap between us—but at least I might have understood you better. Although perhaps it's true that the only way we can learn things is to be told them at the proper time.

I'm glad, though, that you finally let go and told me things about yourself I should have known years ago. You are a fine person, Lisa, and I can only say that I hope you someday meet a man who is man enough for you.

The world is a hell of a mess, isn't it? It's the damnedest thing, the way things never work out right for people. People keep falling in love with each other, or thinking they've fallen in love with each other, or at the very least, falling in bed with each other, and they keep turning out to be wrong for each other and all they really do is fuck up one another's lives.

I'm not speaking for myself at the moment, as my present situation is ideal. Rozanne and I *are* perfect for each other, although I can certainly see how either of us would be quite impossible for any other human being.

As a matter of fact, what brings on this miasma is word I've just had from Steve and Fran. Despite the tone I may have taken in my letters to them—a callow sort of sniping I now see was quite unworthy of me—I really thought Steve and Fran would be right for one another.

You see, Fran left me because I wasn't man enough for her. I knew that at the time, whether or not I wanted to admit it to anyone, myself included. And I knew she certainly wouldn't have that problem with Steve Adel. I don't know how much you know about Steve, but the one thing that was always a sore point in our otherwise ideal friendship was that I envied him his manhood. There's an inner strength about him, not always evident at first glance, that is really awesome.

Few women notice this right away. Of course, Steve's not the typical make-out artist. It takes a special sort of woman, a strong sure-of-herself woman, to attract him in the first place. He was never the type to bother with round-heeled pushovers. Mattress girls, he would call them, though not without a certain degree of sympathy.

I thought Fran had met her match in Steve, and while I may have begrudged them their happiness, I also envied them.

What I never stopped to realize was that, this time, it was Fran who was overmatched.

He turned out to be literally too much for her.

Isn't that irony of the most bitter sort? Fran's in New Mexico now, living with a widowed aunt and thinking of entering a convent. Thinks all men are beasts because she finally experienced a real man. And Steve's stuck in Cuernavaca because she ran off with all his money, and anyway he has no place to go. From his letter, he sounded pretty miserable. I gather he hasn't met anybody interesting. All sorts of available broads, but he was never the type to waste his time on available broads.

Who would have thought it would end this way?

Well, enough of this outpour of melancholy. Once again, I'm glad I've taken the time to work it all out on the old typewriter. I owe the Messrs. Smith and Corona a monumental debt. I've shaken the mood, and I only hope the result won't be to shove you down into a depression. I still believe that there's a right person for every person, and though it may seem Pollyannaish to say it, I'm sure the day will come when you'll find the man that's right for you. And perhaps one day even Steve will find a woman equal to him.

Got to cut this short. Jennifer's coming over for dinner *à trois*, and I want to get this in the mail before she arrives.

In haste,

Larry

Mrs. Laurence Clarke
c/o Kettleman
14 Fairfax
Albuquerque, New Mexico

Dear Fran:

I can't begin to tell you how sorry I am for you. Yet, in a way, I'm glad that things turned out as they did, because you know now that life with Steve would have been utterly impossible for you. In that sense, Fran, it's a damned good thing you found out as soon as you did. Imagine if you had married him. Imagine, if you will, if you had had children by him!

You know, I almost blame myself. Steve was my friend, and I have this loyalty thing that renders me blind to a friend's faults. Even when I'm aware of them, I don't let on to others.

If not for this, you never would have started an affair with Steve. I could have told you, for example, that the guy has a Nietzschean attitude toward women. You know the passage in *Zarathustra* about women being like dogs? The more you beat them, the more they love you? He used to walk around quoting that in college.

To put it bluntly, the man is a sadist. I don't know what the brute did to you, but I can make a pretty good guess. If I'm right, you would never have had to worry about getting pregnant.

Well, let's not dwell on unpleasant things. Although you're absolutely right that our marriage is over—and was over, in many respects, well before you first started sleeping with Steve—I still feel responsible for your welfare. Maybe responsible is the wrong word for it. I care for you, Fran, and I'd like to see you get yourself back on the right track. An affair right now would be the worst thing for you, you're dead right about that, but at the same time it's not going to do you any good moping around with some old aunt in Albuquerque.

May I make a suggestion? I think what you need is some time in the open air, time to think, time to relax, time to reactivate your old interest in horseback riding under a clear and unpolluted sky. And, coincidentally enough, there's a place right near where you are now that I happen to know of, and I can't think of any spot in the world that would be better for you.

It's the Bar-Bison Dude Ranch, and the mailing address is Altamont, New Mexico. Unlike so many resorts where you would have men constantly chasing after you, this is a genuinely relaxing place. Do me a favor. Hell, do yourself a favor. The minute you put down this letter, pick up the phone and call Bar-Bison and make a reservation. And go there right away.

I promise you it'll do you a world of good.

Larry

c/o Gumbino
311½ West 20th St.
New York 10011
July 26

Miss Mary Katherine O'Shea
and Miss Barbara Judith Castle
Bar-Bison Dude Ranch
Altamont, New Mexico

Toothsome Merry Cat and Succulent B.J.:

I am enclosing some correspondence from and to my wife, Fran. I think these letters are self-explanatory. Perhaps the summer will turn out to be more entertaining than you may have guessed.

Ellen was here recently and sends you both her love. Alison is due shortly with what she describes as an erotic painting for our apartment. And I had a letter the other day from Dawn and Naughty Nasty Nancy. It looks as though Camp Whatchamacallit is working out well, although Dawn had a fairly hysterical scene with a lifeguard. But rather than spoil it, I'll let her tell you herself when she sees you.

While nothing's certain in this vale of tears, I think you can expect a visit from my wife before long. You professed to wonder what she was like, and now I think you'll be able to find out. The name *Merry Cat* may be familiar to her, so herself might start calling herself just plain *Mary*, and B.J. can get used to *Barbara*. We all have to make occasional sacrifices.

Oh, hell, I don't have to teach you angels how to scheme. Like teaching birds how to fly.

The ball's in your court, kittens. Have fun.

Uncle Larry

BAR-BISON DUDE RANCH
ALTAMONT
NEW MEXICO

"Where Nothing's Barred Except The Bison"

August 8

c/o Gumbino
311½ West 20th St.
New York 10011

Hi, Uncle Larry!

This is secret agent Barbara speaking. Say hey, next time you give the Dolly Sisters an assignment, make it a tough one. We were all excited and couldn't wait for your better half (hardly!) to get here. We kept hatching one outrageous plot after another and secret agent Mary would whisper something to me and we would both burst into a fit of hysterical laughter and before long they were all giving us funny looks. Even the horses thought we were crazy.

And they were *right!*

All seriousness aside, Uncle-Poo, we checked the registrations and saw she was really coming and really started in hatching schemes, figuring that this would be a real test of our Notorious Powers of Seduction.

And then there was nothing to it.

Larry, that woman is a lesbian. That woman managed to live twenty-nine years of her life without ever suspecting the truth, and it evidently took a cock up her ass to give her the idea, or at least that was what she kept talking about, how men give you sweet talk and pretend to be in love and all they want to do is bugger you and split your asshole open. Of course she found a more genteel way to say it, but that was what it added up to.

Merry Cat made the original pitch. She started off telling Fran how she didn't like the way all the cowboys bothered her (which they don't, the schmucks are all either faggots or else they just want to marry rich divorcees, or both) and Fran came right back with a line about how men are all beasts, and from then on it was almost a question of who was going to seduce whom.

Merry Cat wants to tell you the rest of it, so I'll say *au revoir*. "*Au revoir.*" There, I said it. Your turn now, Mary Katherine.

B.J.

This is Mary Katherine O'Shea speaking. Talk about insatiable dykes! She was here for a week and wouldn't leave us alone. She ate all her meals between our legs. I'm not kidding, Larry. It's the truth.

Do you remember the other letter you wrote us? Telling us not to worry that we were lesbians? I think we may have been ready to do a wee bit of worrying in spite of what you said, but the week with your spouse really set us straight. Ooops! Sorry about that.

But it did. That woman is a dyke and she's as different from us as, oh, night and day, since I can't think of anything more original just at the moment. She has this hangup where all she can talk about is how rotten men are. By the time she was ready to leave, it really got to me. I felt like going out and fucking one of the horses.

I'll bet she never fucks a man again as long as she lives.

She talked about Steve quite a bit, and also about you, and it was slightly weird pretending we never heard of any of you people before, but she never caught on, even when B.J. slipped and told her what school we were from. It didn't even register. She didn't say much that was interesting, except one time she said, "Larry knew about me all along. He used to pester me to find out if I ever made it with a girl. I guess it was always obvious to him."

Oh, one other thing. She's going to divorce you, but she's into this Women's Lib thing to such a degree that she won't accept alimony because it destroys a woman's dignity. I don't suppose that will make you shed tears!

Send us more assignments from time to time. We love our work, and we love you.

Sister Mary Katherine, S.J.

Cuernavaca

Mr. Laurence Clarke
c/o Gumbino
311½ West 20th Street
New York, New York

Lorenzo, mi amigo—

You're not going to believe this. Damn it all, you are simply not going to believe this.

I'm getting married in the morning. Here, in glorious Cuernavaca. Me. Steve. Your old buddy, the permanent bachelor.

And it's all your fault, you sweet old sonofabitch.

That's not the part you're not going to believe, although God knows it's unbelievable enough. The capper is that I'm getting married to Lisa. Your ex-wife. *That* Lisa.

Well, in this case you can't be pissed, can you? I mean, I waited until you were done with her before I picked up on her. You can't be pissed this time.

As far as I'm concerned, you're Thomas Edison and Marconi and all those cats rolled into one. Because I took your advice again, Larry, and this time I made it work. Turned her on but good, flipped her over, rammed it halfway to her small intestine, and pinned her steady while I pumped it to her.

Screamed her head off. I thought we would have Mex cops all over the bed. But I kept it up just the way you said, and lo and goddam behold, Larry, if it didn't work like a charm.

Fantastic. She's got big tits and a rich father and she worships the fucking ground I walk on. Keeps telling me I'm the only genuine man in a world full of faggots. All I have to do is look at her and she melts.

Now I know how God feels.

Your pal forever,
Steve

Cuernavaca

Dear old Larry,

I'll bet when you got a letter with all these flashy Mexican stamps on it, the last thing you expected was a letter from your ex. But that's what this is.

And that's not the greatest surprise, either.

Lover, you're not going to believe this. You're just not going to believe it. But every word of it is true.

I'm not just your ex-wife anymore. I'm also the wife of your best friend. Just five hours ago as I write this, I was married to Steve Adel in a tacky little church a few blocks from where we're staying.

It's your fault, of course. That letter you sent me put a bee in little Lisa's bonnet. I had to find out if Steve was everything you said he was. Kiddo, you didn't half do him justice! I suppose it's the height of something or other to praise your husband to your ex-husband, but I have trouble restraining myself, I'm just all bubbly inside.

If I were the type to write obscene letters, like a certain former husband of mine, I could write a scene that would burn out your retinae. But that's a memory I want to keep to myself. I won't share it with you or anyone else.

Consider yourself richer to the tune of $850 a month. And consider yourself thanked—without even meaning to, you did me the greatest favor of my life.

Now and forever,
Mrs. Stephen Joel Adel

c/o Gumbino
311½ West 20th St.
New York 10011
August 15

Mr. Roland Davis Caulder, Esq.
Muggsworth, Caulder, Travis & Beale
437 Piper Blvd.
Richmond, Va.

Dear Mr. Caulder:

Permit me to congratulate you on having one less blood-hound in your kennel!

I refer, in my usual chatty way, to the marriage of your daughter Lisa Beth Caulder Clarke to the estimable Stephen Joel Adel of Centre Street, New York. I can honestly say that the news came as no surprise to me, for it seems to me that the union of these two fortunate lovers is not a mere happenstance but the manifestation of some Master Plan.

I'm happy, of course, and my happiness goes beyond the cessation of my obligation to keep your little bloodhound bitch in Alpo. And I trust you too are happy to see the Davis and Caulder lines enriched by that of the famous name of Adel. Surely you, as a breeder of fine dogs, can appreciate the need to introduce an outside bloodline from time to time, and God knows the Davises and Caulders have inbred of late to the point of idiocy.

Look at the bright side, sir. You haven't gained a son-in-law, you've unloaded a daughter.

Unfortunately, this means the end of our personal correspondence. I'm sure this grieves you as much as it grieves me. I trust, though, that we will be able to renew our acquaintance at blessed occasions. For my part, I look forward to seeing you at your grandson's birth, and, God willing, at his bar mitzvah.

Very truly mine,

Laurence Clarke

From the desk of Clayton Finch, President

August 21

Mr. Clayton Finch, Pres.
Whitestone Publications, Inc.
67 West 44th St.
New York 10036

Dear Mr. Finch:

Please forgive my using your stationery. I was going to employ some of my remaining *Ronald Rabbit's* stock, but since the business I have at hand is more that of Whitestone than of the lamented magazine, I felt this would be more appropriate. Also, and I say this not to turn your head, it was my feeling that your own personal letterhead might carry more weight with you.

Just yesterday I was reading through a stack of correspondence written over the past couple of months. Old habits never die, or so they say, and my editorial eye quickly realized that there ought to be a market for this material. My first impulse was to offer it for serialization in the forthcoming *Rachel Rabbit's Magazine for Girls and Boys*, but I felt the nature of certain passages might prove objectionable in certain backward areas of the country.

At that point, a girl I know suggested that this file might make an extraordinary book. I thought it over and decided she was absolutely right. Of course we would have to change names and addresses around somewhat, but that should present only a minor problem. With that exception, we could present the material exactly as written and call it a novel.

I thought at once of you. My loyalties have never faded despite our periodic differences, Mr. Finch, and we all know that Whitestone's paperback division, Hardin Books, needs all the help it can get.

I am thus enclosing copies of all correspondence herewith. You will no doubt be familiar with some of this material—indeed, you are the author of some of it—and for that reason, plus my reluctance to deal with underlings, I thought I would submit directly to you rather than to the Hardin editorial department.

I'll look forward to hearing from you.

With every good wish,

Laurence Clarke

LC/rg
Enc.

WHITESTONE PUBLICATIONS, INC.
67 West 44th Street
New York 10036

From the desk of Clayton Finch, President

August 25

Mr. Laurence Clarke
c/o Gumbino
311½ West 20th Street
New York 10011

Dear Mr. Clarke:

You win. I give up. Contracts follow.

Clayton Finch

CF/jrp

c/o Gumbino
311½ West 20th St.
New York 10011
August 28

Secretary to the President
Whitestone Publications, Inc.
67 West 44th St.
New York 10036

Dear jrp:

You don't know me, jrp, but there's something about the way you type a letter that intrigues me. I was wondering if you would possibly be interested . . .